G000093496

SWANSONG
GM Jordan

Swansong ™ & © 2014 GM Jordan & Markosia Enterprises, Ltd.
All Rights Reserved. Reproduction of any part of this work by any
means without the written permission of the publisher is expressly
forbidden. All names, characters and events in this publication are
entirely fictional. Any resemblance to actual persons, living or dead is
purely coincidental. Published by Markosia Enterprises, PO BOX 3477,
Barnet, Hertfordshire, EN5 9HN. FIRST PRINTING, February 2015.
Harry Markos, Director.

ISBN 978-1-909276-57-4

Editor: Stephanie Holland-Hill

Book design by: Ian Sharman

www.markosia.com

This paperback edition 2015

First published by Markosia Enterprises 2014

For esperer

SPECIAL THANKS

Thanks to my family, Alison Bailey, Karen Wenborn, Alan & Jan Harding, Molly, Susan, the Gough family, Sarah Reynolds, Tim Pilcher, David Morris, David and Karen Lota, Harry Markos, Ian Sharman, Nichola Wilkinson, Paul H. Birch and all the people who have supported me and kicked me when I was on the verge of giving up.

Special thanks to the wonderful Stephanie Holland-Hill without whom this story would never have been edited and fit for reading.

To Paul, I never stopped chasing the dream;
it just kept out running me!

THE END

The light frost of the early morning gave the world a crisp, clean look to it. The hedges lining the road appeared to be made from icing, cobwebs keeping the tiny droplets of water like a million tiny flies.

Slowly a black car pulled into a driveway, the windows heavy with mist shielding the occupants from prying eyes. It pulled up to the house and stopped, a heeled foot stepped lightly onto the gravel and was closely followed by another. Black silk stockings ran under a long coat that was pulled up tightly around the owner's face. She reached into the car and pulled out a small case.

Carefully she made her way to the door and knocked smartly, from the outside it appeared that the house was lifeless, it was if it mimicked her feelings deep inside. A few seconds later the latch was drawn back and the door opened, she stepped inside quickly and the door closed once again.

China didn't pay much attention as she was led down the corridor and into a wood panelled study, she held the case tightly but her coat was removed. Underneath she wore a simple black dress that stopped just above her knees; as was her Master's wishes she did not wear anything underneath except her stockings. Around her neck she wore a simple black leather collar that locked at the back, she had thought about removing it but felt lost without it.

Instinctively she stood with her legs apart, hands behind her back. Subconsciously she leaned back so her ample breasts could be seen. She breathed lightly, the events of the last few days were catching up with her and now she felt tired and alone. She wanted to curl up in a ball in her

Master's lap in safety. Tears fought their way into her eyes but she held them back.

"Master will be along shortly." China looked up and noticed the girl attending to her for the first time. Her hair was cut short and she was pretty, any other time China might have thought her attractive. She wore little more than a rough smock and it was clear to China that the girl was a novice.

She nodded.

"Would you like to sit down, you must be cold and tired?" The girl tried to appear kindly but the cold China felt was not down to the weather.

"Thank you but I prefer to stand."

The girl nodded and left. The door quietly clicked shut and left alone China would normally relax, instead she bowed her head and allowed a single tear to fall down her pale cheek. Closing her eyes she tried to remember how she had felt when she first arrived to start her training, it seemed a lifetime ago.

ONE

Gill knew deep down inside she was made differently. For as long as she could remember her life was busy and prosperous. She was respected and well liked but hidden away was another side that she wanted to explore but couldn't, something lurked in her dreams waiting to be released.

She remembered one Christmas at university when she had been very drunk at a student party. She had blushed as her boyfriend told his friends how great she looked naked playfully slipping down her top as they danced. Everybody cheered as she stood in just a revealing bra in the middle of the room but she hid her excitement from them and pulled her blouse up quickly. Back in her room, lying on her bed she had slipped her hand between her legs and felt how hot she was; within minutes she had climaxed. Gill wasn't sure if it was the thrill of being displayed in public or the applause, but whatever it was she felt alive and more aroused than she had been in her life.

The door clicked shut and brought her back to her senses, her eyes focused on the room and China waited for the new arrival to come into sight, she never moved her head.

A man in his forties walked slowly across the room and poked the fire, greying around the sides his hair was cut short and neat, his silk shirt was immaculate, the jacket he wore would not have looked out of place in the 1930's and his dark trousers danced with the red glow of the fire. Finally he turned to look at her. In the half-light of the room his eyes appeared black, he looked long and hard at China for a moment, judging her soul. "Is it true?" he finally asked. He sat back in the leather seat and crossed his legs. She could do little more than nod, her legs felt like lead and she suddenly felt sick.

"This afternoon, a little after 4pm he slipped away." Deep inside her stomach turned a knot of nerves that got tighter.

"Why have you come to me?" he asked, his fingers made a triangle, the tips touched his lips.

"My Master asked me to give you this." Slowly China reached into the case and handed him a sealed envelope, wax held the edges tight. Slowly the master of the house cut the seal and ran his eyes over the text, it was quite long but he read quickly.

"You are the sole heir to his estate, until such time as it is settled you will remain in my charge."

"Yes Sir," China said slowly, she had expected to be left alone.

"You will call me Master now," he told her, carefully placing the letter into the desk draw.

"I'm sorry, Sir. With respect I cannot do that." She surprised herself with the statement, and was even more surprised when he smiled. He rang the small bell on the desk and within seconds the novice reappeared.

"Take China's case to the room next to yours, she must be exhausted from carrying it." The girl reached for the bag but China was loathe to let go. Finally she conceded and released her grip. She turned to leave.

"Before you go… Is it correct that you wear his mark?"

China slowly raised her dress hem and turned around, her buttocks were firm and red, and she heard his surprise.

"Yes Sir. It is true as you can see." On each cheek sat the tattooed markings of her Master, gothic text held neatly in a neat oval of black.

"I have never seen his mark displayed so permanently."

"He was my Master," she breathed deeply trying to remain calm.

"You will make him proud," the man stated, "or you will answer to me."

"Yes Sir."

TWO

The passages of the house played tricks with her eyes, the light was held low enough that she could walk without fear of falling but could not make out features on the walls or ceiling. She had to keep a brisk pace to keep up with the girl in front, fearful that should the girl move out of sight she might lose her.

Eventually they came to a door and the novice stopped, she turned a key in the lock and pushed the door open, slipping the case down just inside the room. China entered.

The bed itself was large and surrounded by four posts, from which hung heavy curtains. It's seemed too grand for a submissive but she was not going to complain.

"Please put my case on the bed," she asked the girl.

"I'm sorry for your Master's passing but you have no status here. Put the bag up yourself," the girl responded as she faced China.

The slap rang out around the room, it was a shock to both China and the girl and for a second neither was sure where it had come from. A red mark rose on the girl's cheek and her tears flowed.

"Put my case on the bed, now," China found herself ordering, seconds later her case sat neatly on the side of the bed. "You may go."

As the door closed on the departing girl China found her entire world was gone, she was alone, more alone than she had ever been and she started to cry.

Gill sat on a leather sofa and watched people milling around, the art on the walls didn't particularly interest her but the champagne was cold, the music was good and she didn't have anywhere else to go on a Saturday night. Her eyes wandered, drifting across the faces of the people crowded into the recesses looking at the drab artworks hanging on the white walls. She thought briefly about her husband, she had thought they were happy but then one day she came home from work to find his clothes gone, the deeds to the house sat on the table and signed over to her. This was his kind of event, his world not hers.

As she drifted into her own thoughts her eyes strayed to the far corner of the room where several people stood around a large chair. Her eyes met the occupant. He filled the space. She noted his hair was red-brown, cut short and away from his face, and she couldn't stop looking at his eyes, deep and almost black. He had a strange shaped beard that was cut high on his cheeks, dark against his pale complexion.

By his side a girl sat upright, her skirt was cut short, a black mesh top was almost transparent and her breasts were clearly visible under the lights of the gallery. Her legs were open and she rested her hands in her lap, Gill noted her make-up, bright red lips, her eyelids were darkened in such a way as her blue eyes seemed dazzling. Finally her hair was pulled back tightly, she looked stunning and Gill felt the heat rising between her legs. Occasionally she watched the girl rise and return with another drink for her partner but she never drank herself unless he held the glass for her, then her mouth would eagerly close over the rim, she never lost her elegance and throngs of men strolled over. They would talk to the stranger but look at his companion, their eyes flicking over every part of her, but when it became clear she was not interested in them they would wander away uncomfortably only to be replaced by another,

At the end of the evening Gill kissed her host goodbye and stood on the street waiting for her taxi, the lights of the city danced off the Thames and she watched them for a minute. A car drew up, and she watched as the couple from the Gallery walked out. The woman opened the door and the man stepped inside, turning to look Gill in the eye. She felt her heart pounding as he appeared to look deep inside her and long since buried feelings surged through her body and mind. He held the look as the woman stepped into the car and finally closed the door.

Shaking, Gill climbed into her taxi when it arrived, her hand rested on her thigh and she longed to stroke herself. Slowly she slipped her dress up her thighs. The taxi driver watched her in his rear view mirror as she closed her eyes, her fingers slipping inside her jacket and gently squeezed her breasts, pinching her nipples.

Her legs opened wide as she remembered the look on the girl's face of contentment and desire. Gill felt hotter, she was getting wetter as his eyes jumped into her thoughts, amazing eyes that undressed her and made her feel like a student again being watched by the crowd.

Almost unconsciously she let out a deep sigh. Seconds later she was aware that strange fingers caressed her inner thigh, she snapped open her eyes and stared at taxi driver. They had pulled into a quiet street and he grinned at her- she wanted to close her legs but the need to be touched stopped her. Wantonly she opened them further and slipped her dress higher revealing her stocking tops. His fingertips brushed her gusset, teasing her lips through the silk material.

"Come into the front," he ordered, grinning. She tried to resist, looking out the windows to see if anyone was around. When it was clear they were alone she stepped out of the back and into the passenger seat.

His cock was already out of his trousers when she sat down; she shook her head and tried to open the door but his hand flicked out and gripped her wrist.

"Show me your titties." His voice was demanding and coarse; she felt afraid but slowly unbuttoned her jacket and blouse. Roughly he reached out and mauled her soft breasts through her bra. She moaned and then hated herself for enjoying it.

"You like that, don't you."

She shook her head and tried to be defiant, pushing herself back against the door and trying to break his touch. But he changed tact and ran his fingers up her thigh, she felt his rough hands over her stockings and wanted to run away, wide-eyed her legs opened to his touch and within seconds he was pushing his fingers inside her panties.

"You're very hot, you want this don't you?" She shook her head at his statement. "Boy, you are such a dirty bitch playing with yourself in the back of my cab. I'll make you a dirtier bitch."

His hand gripped the back of her head and pulled her forward. The spell was broken and Gill fought him, desperate not to give in. He was stronger though and pulled her easily into his lap but she clamped her mouth and refused to take his hard cock.

The pain that erupted from her buttocks was both sharp and unexpected as the flat of his hand came down hard against her soft cheeks and took her breath away.

"Dirty little bitches that don't do what they are told are spanked," he spat as he continued to spank her, her cheeks got hotter and hotter. She could feel the heat rising between her legs, she was desperate for him to stop and touch her, she needed to be fucked.

"Pllllllllllllleaaaaaase," she moaned, "please stop and I'll do what you want." She opened her mouth and took his salty cock into her mouth, greedily sucking him deep into her throat. As he relaxed his grip it became apparent that he wasn't going to touch her so Gill slipped her hand between her legs and stroked herself. Through the material she could feel her clit throbbing, she was desperate for more but she felt the cock jerk in her mouth and pulled back, his climax spilled over her lips, a second load landed on her cheek and she turned her face.

He released his grip and let her sit up, she could smell his sweat and sperm, it made her sick to think what she had just done. Her buttocks were burning and she grabbed her bag and tumbled out onto the pavement desperate to put distance between them. The taxi started up, the engine turning over for a second before he drove off. She watched him driving off before putting her clothes straight and walking towards the main road.

The thoughts of the Saturday night weighed in her mind as she tried to work - the image and smell of the driver were gone and all she could feel was the hardness of his hand and the eyes of the stranger in the galleries. When she closed her eyes to sleep she could feel him watching her.

Eventually she picked up the phone and dialled the number of the party organiser, she listened to the phone ringing and wondered if she should hang up but eventually the machine answered it.

"Mary, hi, just wanted to thank you for the party the other night. I was wondering, there was a big guy there with a very distinctive beard with his girlfriend sitting to one side. I know his face from somewhere – could you let me know who he is?" She put down the phone and swivelled in her chair. London spread out in front of her; somewhere out there he was working.

THREE

For two days Gill worked, ate and slept on automatic pilot, the urge she had first felt come to the surface at University was stronger now and she knew it had something to do with the punishment she had felt at the hands of the taxi driver. She just couldn't shake the eyes of the stranger – it all seemed mixed up in one and it was driving her crazy.

Finally a card arrived at her office by messenger, it was small and a little bit bigger than a business card – she recognised Mary's handwriting and ripped the envelope open eagerly. It was black; in the centre were simply the words 'Master J', a telephone number and e-mail address. Slowly she turned it over expecting more, but there was nothing.

All she could do was look at the information on the card and wonder – the mystery was getting deeper but at least she had a name to go with the face. When the phone rang she nearly jumped out of her thoughts.

"Hello, Gill," – she recognised the voice at the end of the line instantly.

"Hi Mary, I got the card."

"So you were attracted to him?" Mary asked, teasing her old friend.

"Not really, but there was something about him that was familiar. How do you know him?" Gill pushed, eager to learn more.

"Meet me at the Metropol Hotel, 8pm. Be prompt and I'll leave a message at reception where you can find me," the telephone went dead and Gill look a little surprised. She called back but got no reply.

The Metropol was quiet, although the restaurant seemed busy and a couple of American tourists checked in but the main body of the hotel seemed lifeless. Gill walked over to the reception desk and gave her name; the concierge gave her a note but said nothing. Hooked by the situation she found a seat in the reception area and opened the note, she read it twice 'Wait for me, when you see me go to the lifts give me fifteen minutes and come to room 415, there is a key in the envelope. Come into the room, take a seat but do not say a word.'

She fished into the envelope and pulled out the cardkey. Turning it over in her hands she waited, feeling nervous and a little sick again but couldn't leave. A little after eight she watched Mary walk from the bar, she wore a long coat, tights or stockings and black heels. The coat was tied tight at the front and she held the top protectively. Gill looked down at her watch and as Mary disappeared into the lift she made a note of the time and settled back.

The next fifteen minutes dragged and Gill found the palms of her hands were sweating – she sat with her legs crossed and gently tapped her knee. Nervously she looked around at the people coming and going and once or twice she caught the concierge looking at her but a simple smile sent him scuttling off to do something else. Eventually the watch hands told her it was time to move and she stood up, crossed the reception area and pressed the lift button. When it slid open she stepped inside quickly and selected the right floor, desperate to be the only person in the car.

She smoothed her clothes as she rode the lift up into the unknown – she crossed and uncrossed her hands and became desperate for the toilet, a ball of nerves had built up in her stomach and she wondered if she was doing the right thing. When the doors opened she nearly jumped out of her skin. She stepped onto the burgundy carpet and walked the corridor slowly until she found 415. The key slipped into the lock easily and she turned the handle.

Gill found the room to be large, almost a suite. The main area was dominated by a space of about eight square feet square, in the centre of which a chair had been placed. To one side a small table was arranged with various riding crops and paddles, chains and bars. Torquemada would have been hard pressed to find a use for some of the instruments. Her heart was in her mouth as turned to leave, her hand reaching for the door handle when a small cough span her around. The girl from the gallery stood before her, champagne in her hand.

"Please feel free to sit, a chair has been arranged for you to one side," she stated simply. Gill followed her into the room and sat in the corner.

The entire room was visible from where she sat; she drank nervously from the glass and waited. Music played in the background and Gill took the time to look the girl over. She was dressed in much the same way as when Gill had seen her in the gallery and stood with her arms behind her back, legs apart with her head up. In the light of the room Gill could see she wore no make-up and was still beautiful – Gill could see why the men couldn't keep their eyes off her.

Through the top it appeared her nipples were pierced, something Gill hadn't seen in the Gallery. She wondered if this woman, girl, was 'Master J's' girlfriend or wife and why she adopted such a posture of almost total submission. Before she could think of possible answers to the questions the stranger stepped into the room from the bedroom. He crossed the room almost stiffly and spoke in a whisper to the girl, who nodded her head and went into the bedroom.

"I must apologise, it would appear that Mary is a little unsure of herself tonight. Please forgive me." His voice was deep but gentle and he seemed a little whiter than the last time she had seen him. Gill found she was unable to match the accent with the face, it seemed out of place but she smiled.

"Maybe I should leave; this is obviously a moment that needs to be private." Gill went to stand but the bedroom door opened and Mary walked into the room. The mask she wore was made of black satin with thin threads disappearing into her red hair. She crossed the room and knelt in front of J, her legs remaining open, hands sat neatly in the small of her back.

Mary wore black stockings, a small black thong and a bodice that pushed her breasts up until they nearly spilled over the top. Her breathing was heavy and laboured and around her neck a tatty brown collar rubbed her pink skin.

J lifted her face and looked into her eyes, "Why have you come to me?" His voice had changed, it was more commanding and stern and shivers rolled down Gill's spine; goose bumps rose on her skin.

"I ask that you train me, guide me, make me your slave. I wish to serve you." Mary's voice was timid and shaky, she shook uncontrollably. Gill felt a flush of excitement run through her body.

J ran his fingers down her face, the backs of his fingers caressed her skin softly and he peered into Mary's eyes.

"No you have come to me for absolution, for another purpose. You do not wish to serve and I cannot train you." The softness returned to his voice and he waited for her to speak.

"Please, I need to be punished. You must punish me," Mary begged. Gill caught her breath at the words- when she remembered to breathe again she found the girl standing by her side pouring more Champagne.

"What's happening?" she whispered into the girl's ear.

"Your friend is a fashion victim, the Master can feel she is no real submissive and has no tolerance for timewasters," came the soft reply. "Watch."

Gill could no longer pull her eyes from the scene unfolding before her.

"Very well, you will be punished," he walked to the chair and rested his hands on the back, Gill was sure she caught a flash of pain in his eyes for a second but then it was gone. She watched as he took a paddle in his hands and ran his palm over it.

"Crawl to me. When you reach me stand up and turn around, place your hands on the back of the seat. Keep your legs straight, knees 12inches apart and back straight."

In horror Gill watched her friend crawl on hands and knees to J's feet, her face inches from his shoes; she stood slowly and bent as instructed. Mary's cheeks were round and pink, her curves highlighted by the thong that separated them.

"The bar." He said simply. The other girl walked to the table and lifted a spreader bar, placing it between Mary's legs and opening the recipients' legs a little wider so it fitted.

"That was a twelve inch bar. You did not do as you were told, another three strokes," the tip of the crop tapped a ball-gag on the table and Gill sat fascinated as it was placed in Mary's mouth and fastened at the back. Desire flowed through Gill's body, desire for the care and attention J paid to Mary, desire to serve in the same way the girl did.

"Mary has not told me what she requires punishment for, but she will take nine strokes of the crop for it, and another three for not doing as she has been told," he explained to Gill, bending the crop aggressively, swishing it through the air to test it.

Gill sat in the room and tried to believe what she had seen. She shook and was sure she was as white as a sheet – to her horror she had witnessed the chastisement of her friend with a crop designed for an animal, the red welts marked the tender flesh in a burning ladder. She heard the cries of pain and had seen Mary jerk with every lash. When it was over she watched as the mask was removed, tears ran in streams down her puffed face, but almost unbelievably she heard Mary whisper, "Thank-you, Sir," as the gag was removed from her mouth.

J walked uncertainly towards the bedroom and allowed the girl to remove the bar without him. Mary remained in the same position, waiting to be allowed to move. For several minutes only the girl moved until eventually J returned. He had removed his jacket and when he smiled at Gill she melted in his eyes.

"When did you sleep with Gill's husband, Mary?"

The words were like a gunshot ringing around the room.

"What?" Gill stammered, unsure of what she had heard.

Mary burst into tears, and seemed more pitiful than when she was taking her punishment, "How did you know… please don't."

The words seemed hollow, they numbed Gill to the bone and she couldn't move, struck down by their meaning.

"You wished for punishment, I am giving it to you," J stated, he nodded at the girl and she guided Mary down onto her knees again, her sobbing filled the room.

"I'm so sorry; I didn't mean it to happen. Forgive me." She turned her head so she could see Gill, her eyes pleading for forgiveness.

Slowly Gill stood and walked from the room, she didn't shake any more, she simply felt sick and needed fresh air.

FOUR

The Somerset countryside was fresh and pleasing, the new house was everything Gill had wanted as a girl and worked hard for. She was sweeping her old life away and starting afresh even if she was not sure it was what she wanted. The infidelity of her ex-husband and friend although not forgotten was no longer a painful memory. Hate had turned to annoyance but nothing else. More prominent was the memory of seeing Mary punished in such a demeaning manner – she was still not sure how J had known about the affair but she felt that he had the ability to look inside the soul. The memory of him made goose bumps rise on her skin again.

That night as she sorted through her diary his card fell onto the kitchen table; slowly she picked it up and found herself turning it over in her hands. Once again she found herself nervously holding the phone but this time it was the number on the card she dialled; the phone rang for a short time and then a message let her know it had been discontinued. She felt silly, it had been six months so he was sure to have moved on, but as she sat at her computer the wording on the card haunted her and she wrote a simple e-mail which read:

"You gave me the truth, I need to be punished in order to lay the past to rest and to move on. Are you available?"

For a couple of minutes she fought the urge to delete it, eventually she poured a large drink and pressed send. An hour later she checked her mail, found nothing and went to bed sure he was gone.

China sank into the bed and pulled the duvet up around her face, it was comfortable and warm but it was not the place for her. She turned onto her side and looked around the furniture, most of which she judged to be antique, others very clever reproductions. In the distance she could hear the ticking of a clock and then the chimes – she tried to count them but she was too tired. Her eyes closed and exhaustion filled her veins, she felt like she was betraying Master by falling asleep but there was nothing she could do, her spirit was willing but the body was drained.

Once or twice she would wake sure somebody was in the room with her, she felt her face brushed by a familiar warmth, hair stroked from her eyes. She stretched out and her hands touched the headboard, legs already open twelve inches, it was instinctive now even in her sleep.

She felt his warm breath on her breasts, the familiar flicking of his tongue as he worked slowly and methodically down her soft body, kissing and biting her skin, she felt loved and wanted, needed. Gradually her mind became a haze between reality and fantasy – she felt her labia puff at his touch, her clitoris exposed as his lips closed around it and he sucked. Unable to move her arms she could only give in to his control – she still pulled at the restraints but they didn't give way, she was locked down, almost panicking as he did what he wished to her.

She tried to breathe but the bed seemed to suck it from her body – her eyes snapped open and she was sure he was between her legs; she tried to speak, to call out to him but all she could do was raise her pelvis as the climax hit her hard, exploding from the epicentre of her body and draining every ounce of energy from her. It seemed to last forever until eventually she fell back into a laboured asleep again.

The e-mail waited for her when she logged on – her heart felt as though it was in her mouth as she read it over and over. He was in York, only four hours away in the car. It seemed unobtainable and she mulled over how she could do it. Eventually she wrote back and asked him to tell her about the training, what would she endure and would it be the same as Mary's punishment?

His reply was almost instant; she was surprised that his reply came back so soon. 'No, you are special. You need to serve.' The words seemed so simple on the screen but they burned into her, finally something inside clicked and she understood.

She wrote back for more instructions, and printed his reply. She placed it on the table and read it three or four times, making sure she understood all that was required of her for the first meeting. She grew nervous at the prospect, finally she had found herself.

Gill had never been to York; she had passed through it on the train but never got out to look around. She took the letter from her pocket and climbed into a cab.

"Travelodge, Piccadilly," she told the driver and settled back to admire the ancient city as they drove through it. Ten minutes later she stepped from the car and checked in, her room was basic but that is all she would need for the next four days.

She slipped out of her clothes and folded them, placing them in her case and closing the lid. She grew apprehensive about the situation, she could feel the heat rising inside, the confusion raging deep down. Leaning back on the bed her index finger slipped between her legs and pressed her clitoris, she couldn't help but stroke gently, the wisp of neat hair tickled her hand and she pressed harder, the warmth and wetness of her lips surprised her and she arched her back in pleasure.

The knock at the door took her by surprise and she looked in the mirror to make sure her hair was straight, wiped her fingers on a towel and took a deep breath. She walked quickly to the door and peered through the eyehole to make sure it was J, he stood back a little and she noted that he didn't have anything, or anyone, with him. She unlocked the door and returned to the centre of the room, bowing her head and kneeling.

J stood over her, lifted her chin and looked into her eyes, "What do you wish from me?"

"I wish to learn, I wish you to train me, and I want to serve," she breathed as he stared into her eyes. He seemed a little harder than the last time they had met and she understood this is what Mary saw.

"Yes you do." The words were unexpected, Gill had expected to be told she was not good enough and that she too would be punished. "Rise."

She did as she was told, conscious that her naked body was on full display – her cheeks were flushed and she played with her hands as he looked her over. J placed his hand between her legs and she sucked in air sharply letting out a small moan as he pressed her lightly.

"You need to shower and shave."

She was startled at his words but followed him into the shower and allowed herself to be shaved; she marvelled at how gently he used the razor, taking care to ensure he didn't nick her.

The shower was hot and Gill turned under the jet, she was not allowed to use scented soap and was aware that J was waiting, but it felt wonderful and she wanted to stay. Eventually the water stopped and she stepped out onto the cold floor. J handed her a towel, she patted herself dry and allowed herself to be led to the centre of the room, a stool sat in front of the mirror and J motioned for her to sit.

"Tie your hair back away from your face," he ordered. She did as he told her exactly. "Now using just the red lipstick paint your lips."

Wide-eyed she applied it thickly, when she finished he handed her a black lip liner.

"Highlight the outline of your lips." She did as he instructed after which he took it from her and handed her eyeliner. "Now blacken your eyelids and use the pencil to draw back a narrow line from the corner of your eye to your ear, about half an inch.

The transformation was almost complete, Gill marvelled at how beautiful her face was with her new make-up – she looked totally different.

"You will always sit with your legs open 12inches at the knees, you will also sit with your head up." She nodded in agreement and waited to be told what to do next. "Take the lipstick and paint your nipples, then circle your areola with the pencil."

Gill's nerves felt on fire as she followed his instructions, aware that he watched every move she made. Finally when he was satisfied that she was ready he told her to close her eyes. She did so, unsure of what was about to happen and as his fingers stroked her cheek gently he leaned into her ear.

"Trust me," he whispered.

Gill felt soft leather being pulled around her throat and instinctively she bowed her head as she felt the collar being tightened. He buckled it at the back, the metal buckle was cold against her skin, and he let go. Gently he lifted her face, placed her hands in the small of her back and made sure her legs were opened the correct distance. When he was happy he stepped back. "Open your eyes."

She looked straight into the mirror and let out a small gasp, she looked so different and yet it felt so natural. J nodded and went to her case. Pulling it onto the bed he opened it without asking her permission. Impassively Gill sat as he pulled out stockings, lifted a dress and laid his choice of shoes on the bed.

"Stand up," he ordered. Gill did as she was told, standing with her legs apart and keeping her hands in the small of her back, it felt awkward but natural. Without thinking she pushed her breasts forward as she had seen before hoping to please him.

"Stockings, heels and then the dress, do not speak unless spoken to and you will address me as 'Sir'. Do you understand?"

Gill nodded and started to dress as instructed, the feel of the stockings as she pulled them up her legs was amazing; she had never felt so special, so beautiful. Suddenly she was aware that her lips were puffing and she was becoming excited – as she picked up the dress she was aware that J had turned and was taking a drink, she watched him pop two pills into his mouth and swallow. Quickly she turned back and slipped into the dress, taking care not to snag the heels of her shoes in the material.

When she had completed the task she turned to show him, he nodded and motioned for her to step forward.

"Tonight you will kneel by my side when I sit down, you will not speak unless I give you permission, others may touch you but you may not climax without my permission. Do you understand?"

His words burned deep inside, she blushed at some of his words but nodded. He smiled at her.

"You will walk two steps behind me, and should I allow you to sit then you will only sit on bare cheeks. Most importantly you have a new name, you will be introduced as 'China', and you will answer only to that name."

The bar was not full, but it wasn't empty. Gill felt herself becoming China as she followed him inside. She walked behind him; her hands behind her back, the fabric of her dress rubbing at her nipples sending waves of pleasure through her body. She breathed deeply and pressed her thighs together when they were forced to stop walking because of the crowd, she knew that she was wet and in danger of climaxing. People turned to look at her but Gill wasn't sure if it was because she looked fantastic or because she was with J.

Finally they stopped at an empty corner. J sat in a leather chair crossed his legs and motioned for a waiter to come over. Gill stood, a little unsure of what to do for a moment and then walked to the side of the chair; she turned, slid her skirt up a little and slipped down onto her knees. In an instant she became China completely.

China opened her eyes and stretched a little, the curtains had been opened and she looked around the room in natural light. Sliding to the edge of the bed she looked at the clock – it was a little after seven a.m. and she had slept later than she had in a long time. She stood carefully and padded across to her case. She popped the lid and selected a simple skirt and blouse – underneath she saw the shirt her Master had wrapped her in. She lifted it to her nose and drank in deep breaths of his scent, she longed for him to be waiting for her and for a second she felt his breath on her bare shoulder.

The door opened and the little slave walked in, she seemed startled to see China up and around.

"Master asked me to check on you," she whispered, she was obviously excited by China.

"What is your name?" China asked as she pulled out the clothes she was going to wear.

"I have no name yet," was the reply.

China looked her up and down; her eyes took in the girl's dress and stance.

"You will help me dress." China gave her the skirt and blouse to hold as she pulled out new stockings, boots and a make-up case.

The girl walked to the bed and made it before laying the clothes out neatly; she turned to watch China and waited for further instructions.

"Run me a bath. What time does your Master usually wake?"

"Seven – he was up early this morning Ma'am." China fixed her gaze on the novice and judged her.

"I am simply China, I am not Ma'am or Mistress, just China." The girl nodded and trotted off to run the bath.

China stared out the window and took in the gardens, it was very spacious. Master did not have a garden although his flat was filled with dragon trees and tropical plants; the lush greenery filled the rooms with oxygen.

"Your bath will be ready in a few minutes, China"

She turned and faced the girl, running the nail on her index finger around the novice's mouth, caressing it gently. She felt the girl shiver with excitement. China leaned forward so her face was close to the girl's. She looked into her eyes and held her position, dragging the second into an eternity before kissing the novice softly.

The soft moan that escaped the girl's lips made China smile, she remembered her first kiss from another woman, the anticipation, the thrill.

The bath was deep and hot, China lay back and closed her eyes to enjoy the sensation of the water lapping at her body. The novice hovered close by, she offered perfumes and soaps but China declined them all. Eventually the girl stopped chattering and excused herself to check on her Master. China smiled and relaxed – her hand pressed the lips of her sex, two fingers pressed her lips, exposing her clitoris to the warmth of the water until she could no longer hold herself back, arched her back, lifted her pelvis to the surface of the water and stroked her clitoris until she climaxed.

Gill watched various people come over to J; they seemed to ignore her as they talked to him. She wondered if she looked pathetic kneeling by his side, her knees were starting to hurt and she longed to stand up.

A woman swept towards them and Gill was bowled over by the outlandish outfit she wore – it seemed to be made up of endless waves of leather and buckles. She made a beeline for J but couldn't take her eyes off Gill as they talked.

"It's so good to see you again, J. Who is this delicious little creature you have brought along?" the Domme purred, Gill blushed slightly.

"Her name is China, I am teaching her." Gill pushed her chest forward, straightening her back.

"Bring her into the back; let's see how delicious she is."

J stood and Gill followed, her transformation was not complete, she was still torn between her old and new name. They walked quickly through double doors and down a small flight of steps, J and the Domme talked like old friends and when they reached another set of doors J turned to face Gill for the first time since they had arrived.

"Do as you are told, do not let me down." He instructed, she nodded and followed them inside.

The world changed around her, there was a heavy scent in the air that seemed to be a mixture of PVC, leather and sweat; Domme's and Dom's chatted in the half light, submissives of every shape and style waited patiently for instructions. It felt like half the room turned to look at them, and for the first time Gill felt like she was being judged openly. She also felt over dressed. As she watched the Dom's she noticed that none of them looked like J – he wore a suit and polo neck jumper, conservative compared to those around them and yet he fitted in perfectly.

In the centre of the room sat a round table cluttered with glasses and bottles. Various chairs had been pulled up and couples chatted excitedly as they approached. J's companion threw her arms out and hugged a small blonde.

"This is the infamous J," she purred. J smiled and shook the woman's hand.

"How wonderful to meet you at last, I have a young slave that is being a bit feisty and I wondered if you could take a look at her sometime?" she asked.

Gill could feel the respect oozing out of the group and she felt glad she was with him, it elevated her spirit.

"This is my new submissive, China," J announced guiding her forward; they looked into her face and admired her make-up.

J leaned into her so his mouth was close to her ear.

"Slip the dress off your shoulders, show them how beautiful your breasts are."

Gill stood rooted to the spot unable to move, she was being told to expose herself to a roomful of complete strangers.

"Do it, now," J pushed. Gill felt her hands slip to her shoulders and eased down the material; it fell down her body and arms, her breasts came into view and when she shrugged the dress fell to her waist.

"Magnificent," one of the sitters said out loud, the voice belonged to a portly man in his fifties. "How long have you had her?"

J turned to look China in the eyes, as the dress had been peeled away so had the remnants of her nine-to-five life, the transformation was complete.

"I think you can safely say I have owned China all her existence," J stated. China felt the rush of heat return between her legs. The dress fell further and then to the floor – her entire body was now on show but she maintained the correct position demanded by her Master.

FIVE

The hotel room seemed barren and quiet compared to the club and China stood motionless as she waited for J to return from the bathroom. He seemed pale and drawn but his eyes sparkled as soon as he looked at her again. She wanted him; she wanted to feel the hardness of his body deep inside her, taking her.

He stood behind her, his fingers trailed down her body and explored her nakedness; she felt his breath on her neck and ached for his touch to become more intimate.

He leaned into her softly, and wrapped his arm around her, she panicked for a moment unsure of what he required of her, then relaxed as he whispered into her ear.

"Hands behind your back, take a deep breath."

China did as she was told, daring to close her eyes as she felt him stroking her stomach tenderly, his fingers brushed her nerves so gently it felt like he was caressing her skin with a feather. When his fingers touched her pubic mound she led out a small sigh and leaned back against his chest.

"Say 'Please'," he murmured.

"Please… God I want you J," his fingers stopped, she opened her eyes and wondered what was wrong.

"You were told to address me as Sir." His voice was hard and controlled, China suddenly felt afraid.

He walked to the stool and sat down to look at her, his eyes burned into her soul; he straightened his legs.

"Come here and kneel over my legs, accept your punishment."

Unable to resist China crossed the room. She stood before him and shook, she just wore her stockings and heels and felt totally exposed.

J guided her down onto his lap and ran his fingers over her soft cheeks, one hand on her back.

"Open your legs correctly," he commanded, she did it instantly.

The first smack struck her cheeks and sent a wave of shock through her body – she fought to remain in the position he demanded as instinct told her to stand up and demand he leave, but the part of her that was China wanted him to stay. The next smack landed on one cheek and each strike alternated between the two until she was sure she had felt five. Her buttocks felt like they were burning as J ran his fingers across the red hot skin before the final strike landed and made contact with both cheeks at the same time.

He held her in the same position for a few minutes as she caught her breath; he removed his hand from her back but instead of letting her stand up J slipped two fingers between her legs, pressing them into her cunt.

"You are very wet, I am impressed you have not climaxed so far," he stated, his other hand stroking her face and turning her head to look at him.

"Who is your Master?" he asked, fixing her with the same look that had melted her before.

"You are," China rasped, trying to control her body. The climax was pushing itself down to her toes, she became desperate to release it.

J let her go and told her to stand – she did so quickly. She trembled with anticipation, clenching her hot buttocks and praying she didn't climax without his permission. Her Master stood slowly and walked to the bed, China remained in exactly the same position.

"You may climax," he told her.

The first wave hit her hard, she had never wanted to orgasm so much. Her body slumped forward a little and she tried so hard to remain on her feet. From behind he wrapped his arms around her, holding her up, his fingers pumping gently at her cunt.

"Again, give it to me."

It was becoming difficult to breathe, China was desperate for air, her legs were buckling and the room was spinning. She could feel her juices running down her thigh and when she thought she couldn't take any more J turned her to the bed and lay her face down, lifting her legs until she knelt on the side of the bed.

Taking her wrists he locked them behind her back, she turned her head to breathe; her heart was pounding and she trembled uncontrollably, whimpering as his fingers explored her exposed cunt.

Seconds later she felt his breath on her lips – his fingers spread her buttocks and he kissed her cheeks before she felt his tongue flicking down towards her sex.

China found herself moaning uncontrollably as his tongue started to work on her labia, the tip curled up and nudged her clitoris sending waves of pleasure inside her. She wiggled as he probed deep inside her - it felt so good but she wanted to feel his cock.

"Please... fuck me, please, Master," she begged as another climax exploded inside her.

China woke in the bath and sponged herself down, the water had become a little chilly and she stepped onto the tiled floor. Gently she padded herself dry and replaced the towel at the end of the bath; she walked naked into the bedroom completely at ease with her nudity, uncaring as to who saw her.

When she sat down the novice stepped forward and brushed China's hair – like a small child watching an adult she never took her eyes off China as she applied her make-up with the utmost care.

"Stockings and then go into my case and bring me the black bag at the bottom," China instructed. She watched the girl walk across the room; she was ill trained and unsure of herself. China knew she would eventually find herself if her master was good.

When she returned China stretched out her legs and allowed the girl to slip on the stockings. She ran her fingers up her thighs to straighten them, smoothing them so they looked perfect. She stood and opened her legs so that the novice was face to face with the older submissive's sex. China read in her face that novice longed to kiss her, to taste the sweet folds of her vagina.

"Open the bag and take out the contents," China instructed. The girl did as she was told and pulled out a fine bone corset. China turned her back on the girl.

"Pull it around my torso; then hook it up at the back," she commanded. The novice's fingers trembled as she carried out the instructions, China could feel her hot breath on the base of her neck.

"What's your real name?"

China turned to look at the girl, she lifted her chin with the tips of her fingers and stared into the young girl's eyes. "My real name is China, it is the name I was given by my Master and he found it deep inside me, buried by convention."

The girl looked confused and turned away; her fingers ran over the fine clothing in China's case.

"Why China?" she asked. China ran her fingers through the girls hair and stroked her ear.

"It is the name that he found inside me when he unlocked my desire and need."

Gill stirred in the hotel bed and felt J's arm under her neck. She snuggled down onto it and kissed his wrist. As he stirred his other hand rested across her hip and his fingers stroked her soft stomach.

Instantly she was hot and flushed again, parting her legs in the hope that he would move lower. Gently J kissed the back of her head and ran his hand up her body towards her breasts; she rolled onto her back without thinking and pushed her breasts up to meet his fingers. Lazily he ran his fingers around her nipples, rolling them between his finger and thumb before moving from one to the other. Remembering her position Gill stopped herself from stretching out and stroking herself, instead she waited in anticipation as J explored her body at his own pace - every fold and curve was stroked and touched. The heat was rising deep inside her body and she was becoming more aroused than she had ever been in her life.

Closing her eyes Gill realised that she would do anything he asked of her – there was no turning back, she was totally at his mercy and it felt good, natural.

"Put your hands up, grip the headboard," he instructed. "Close your eyes." Gill did as she was told. The wooden struts felt cold against her hot palms; she felt J leave the bed and wondered what was about to happen to her. Minutes later her wrists were encased with soft leather, she tried to pull away from the headboard but found herself unable to move more than a couple of inches. In confusion she twisted her body. He didn't need to restrain her because she would do anything he asked but J's hands gripped her ankles and he looked into her eyes. Gill stopped struggling, melting into his gaze.

"Open your legs, take a deep breath, and relax," he instructed – she nodded, biting her lip.

Watching him intently she could only murmur in pleasure as he started to stroke up her legs with his fingertips, his thumbs making small, tight circles on her skin.

"You play so hard, act so tough but I can feel the real you… hard as rock when you need to be, yet as brittle as bone china." J stated it as a fact, and now she knew he could read her like a book.

"I know what you desire, what you need, but you must do everything I tell you to achieve it. Do you agree?" he asked.

"Yes, Sir," Gill hissed. With every inch he was erasing the parts of her that were old, leaving a void filled with desire and confusion.

Finally his fingers reached her cunt and she struggled to move further down the bed to press harder. He resisted the urge to touch her and instead ran his fingers under her thigh and pressed her anus. It was her first experience of this – it was uncomfortable and a little painful but she didn't complain. Gill closed her eyes opened herself to him.

Her eyes snapped open as she felt his lips sucking gently between her legs, his hand drew back the hood of her clitoris and the very tip of his tongue pressed her button. Electricity poured through her body and she bucked uncontrollably, fighting hard not to climax as he started to hum softly. The vibrations tormented and tortured her, Gill pulled down hard in desperation, eager to feel him inside her boiling cunt.

"Jesus… Nooooooo!" she cried as his finger pushed inside her anus – the climax hit violently and forced the breath from her body.

"Your name?" he asked coolly, pumping her with a steady rhythm.

"CHINA. My name is China… MASTER." Suddenly her legs were shaking uncontrollably and tears poured down her face – despite all the pain and frustration she suddenly felt reborn. J started to drink from her body, his lips hungry for her juices and he expertly curled his tongue to scoop out her nectar. Unable to move China could only ride the waves of climax as they washed over her.

Finally J stopped, tenderly caressing her face as she breathed heavily, fighting to calm down. When he released her from her bindings all China could do was curl in a ball but he turned her over so that she was almost in his lap and stroked the hair from her face.

SIX

Breakfast was taken in a small conservatory at the rear of the building which seemed out of character with the rest of the house.

China turned down the offer of food and stared out the windows across the grounds, trees and bushes bathed in the warming air. Surprisingly the sun was quite strong and was vanquishing all signs of the heavy frost from the night before. She heard footsteps and turned her face to the door. The master of the house strode in, a riding crop in his hand.

"You slept well?" he asked firmly, sitting down and pouring himself a coffee. His actions seemed out of place, China served her Master and had expected the young novice to do the same for hers.

"Thank you, yes. I felt like I could have slept for a week, I guess that everything is finally catching up with me."

He nodded his head and raised the cup to his lips, tiny swirls of steam rose into the air.

"You are welcome to stay as long as you like, it seems a little early to ask you if you have plans for the future."

"I really haven't had time to think." She poured herself a drink and fought the tears that had started to well inside, she was stronger than the emotion; Master had made her stronger and demanded that she not give in.

"The Hunt Ball is in ten days, I shall arrange for a ticket for you. You will, of course, come as my guest and under my protection."

"Thank you, Sir. It may well be the distraction I need."

During the afternoon China strolled in the grounds – she found the playroom easily enough and took the time to run her fingers over the leather straps and metal shackles. She knew her Master had used crops and canes on other submissives he had trained but never on her. Her punishments had been as severe as lashes with the cat, but they burned mentally. He had humiliated her on occasion when she had dug her heels in but allowed her free reign to the point most Dom's would have snapped and then shown her exactly who was in control with simple demonstrations of power.

"I will always be with you." The voice came from behind her and chilled her to the bone, it was familiar but distant.

"What am I going to do Master, you left me?" tears choked in her eyes and she fought the urge to turn around in case the magic failed and she found herself alone. A lump rose in her throat.

"I didn't want to, My Sweet China. Do you think I would chosen to have left the one person I waited my whole life for?" His voice bore into her, numbing her soul.

"But it's unfair. You didn't teach me all I need to know, you didn't teach me what I have to do now." It was anger that replaced the sorrow and she cursed herself for feeling bitter.

"You know how to survive, all I did was to help uncover the part of you that was lost," he stated.

In frustration China lashed out with her hand and knocked crops and canes from a table, rounding on the voice.

"If you loved me then you would have fought harder." Tears poured down her face.

"Because I loved you I fought harder than I had ever done in my life. It's time for you to move on, take control of your life and make me proud." The words were distant and faded into the sunlight.

"Don't leave me," China fell to her knees and cried into her hands.

"Who are you talking to?" The novice startled her and China rose.

"Nobody, myself. Leave me."

"Master asked me stay with you, make sure you were ok," she pressed.

"I told you to leave me." China hoped that when she was alone he could come back to her, explain more.

"You cannot ask me to disobey Master's wishes."

China picked up a paddle and turned it over in her hands, the leather handle was shaped like a penis.

"I'm asking you to obey my wishes – which of us scares you the most?" China asked walking towards the girl. Wide eyed with fear the novice weighed up the question.

"Please, you wouldn't have disobeyed your Master!" China gripped her wrist and pulled her over wooden frame, the girl struggled but China was stronger, her hand pressed down into the girls back and made her bend.

"If you stand up I will spank you harder and longer," China explained, a wide leather strap stretched over the young slaves back and held her down. Expertly the older woman lifted the hem of the smock her victim wore; exposing a neat ladder of cane strokes.

"Legs apart… deep breath," she commanded.

With the first smack the girl tried to break free, hands clawing at the leather strap. Taking heavy iron shackles China locked them around the girl's wrists and fastened them to the legs of the frame.

Gripping the girl's hair she pulled up her face. "You will learn," she hissed.

Work was difficult – every time China closed her eyes or drifted off she replayed the events of the weekend in her mind. Twice on the first day back she found herself locking the door to the bathroom, her fingers snaking inside her panties to bring relief to her aching body. When she woke the next day she resolved to take extra panties to work and to put him out of her mind, it was all well and good finding herself but she had a job to do.

Voices drifted across the office and it took a second for the China to realise that one of the office assistants was talking to her.

"So what did you get up to at the weekend, Gill?" It was a simple question but it didn't register in her mind, it was her name but felt wrong.

"Nothing much, went to York. Visited a friend," she mumbled looking out the window.

"God you look a bit hot, if you're not feeling well then you should go home. I'm sure there's a bug going round and you keep nipping to the loo, why don't you go home we can manage."

China nodded, she needed a shower and sleep, she felt weak fighting the daydreams.

"Call if there are any problems – I will be back the day after tomorrow, there is that big meeting in London tomorrow and I'll go straight there instead of coming in," she grabbed her coat and pulled it on, making her way out the door.

When she reached her car China leaned back into the plush seats and opened her legs, her hand pressed her sex through the material of her skirt but it only served to make her feel stickier, her nipples were sensitive, flashes of electricity surged through her heaving breasts.

Reaching down she pressed the autodial on her phone, her Master's number flashed for a second and she placed it on hands free, China was desperate for him to answer, praying that he was home. Finally he answered.

"Master… Master I need you." She forced herself to grip the edge of the seat in a bid to keep control.

"You have been playing with yourself, haven't you?" China felt herself blush, her response was little more than a whisper.

"Yes, Master. I'm sorry Master."

"Have you climaxed?" he asked, his voice was a little unsteady and China wondered if he was pre-occupied.

She shook herself free from her thoughts.

"No Master, I didn't dare without your permission."

There was a pause at the other end of the line and she wondered if he had left her.

"You may cum… NOW." The explosion that ripped her inside was unexpected and instantaneous, she found it hard to breathe, her nails digging into the seat. As the heat rose she rubbed her thighs together and tried to take a breath, it felt like she would pass out at any moment.

"Again…" he ordered, the climax was less intense but still engulfed her body.

"Please, I need to feel you inside me," she begged as shame at the pitiful nature of her situation crept into her mind.

"You may come to me." The words rocked her to the core, unsure if she dare make the trip.

"How?"

"Drive… or maybe you don't want me that much?" To China it felt like a challenge. She slipped the car into gear and headed for the motorway, the north beckoned.

SEVEN

The novice submissive knelt on the floor and sobbed uncontrollably, her legs had buckled underneath her, arms still stretched skywards.

China placed the paddle back on the table and gripped her chin, lifting the girl's face up; her lips were swollen, eyes red from the tears. Gently China kissed the girl, the palm of her hand cupped the girl's breast and she rolled her hard nipple between forefinger and thumb.

"Do you want to please me?" the girl nodded and China slipped her hand down between the novice's legs, expertly running two fingernails along the girl's labia, her index finger circling the clitoris.

"Will you do anything I ask?" she demanded, lifting the finger to her mouth and sucking the stickiness hungrily.

"Anything, please, I'll do anything you want," a smile stretched across China's lips.

"Cum for me," she hissed.

The girl's body bucked wildly at the command, biting her lip and letting blood trickle down. China pressed the split with her thumb and then rubbed it slowly; her eyes never left the girl's face.

"You have never felt that before, does your Master not exercise such control over you?" the girl trembled, her tears soaked into her cheeks and instinctively her own fingers explored the cut on her lip – slowly she shook her head like a naughty child.

"Such a shame," and turning on her heels China left the room.

It was midday by the time China made it to York, for much of the journey her skirt had been pulled as far up her thigh as she dared, her top had become so uncomfortable as it rubbed that she had undone it almost to her waist in an effort to get relief. By the time she drove into the car park she was as nervous as she had been the first time – she checked her watch and sent a text message to say she had arrived.

Minutes passed, she watched the faces of people coming and going from the lift entrance, she wanted so much to see his face in the groups that emerged. Finally her phone let out a small ring and she half expected the message to read that he wasn't coming; 'Close your eyes, keep them closed until I tell you to open them.'

She did as she was told, straightening her clothes first. Minutes ticked by and she wondered if he was joking, if he was having a sick prank at her expense. The door clicked open and a blindfold was stretched across her eyes, she nearly jumped out of her skin at the sudden sound.

Her arm was taken and she was helped from the car, her keys were taken and she heard the car being locked.

"Head down." She was guided into the back of another car and told to lie down. Fear gripped her, she hoped that Master was close and almost straight away she felt his tender caress, China relaxed.

Cold air touched her face and she was half lifted, half guided out of the car. "Trust me," J whispered into her ear as she was guided forward.

She could feel a stone path under her feet, and then she felt warmer as she was led inside.

Within minutes she felt as though she was alone, she turned her head in an effort to pick up any noise, a slight cough came from her right and she clenched and released her fist.

"How do you feel?" J asked. China knew he already understood how she felt.

"I had to see you, Master, I am so tired and I cannot get you out of my mind." She suddenly felt him kissing the back of her neck, his fingers lifted the hem of her skirt and then slipped into the waistband of her panties.

"Open your legs correctly, keep your back straight." He slipped down the panties and she stepped out of them smartly.

China took a sharp breath and then relaxed as cool air circulated around her sex, she heard the sounds of another person and was aware that they could see her; blushing China tried to slow her breathing and remain calm. Nailed fingers raked across China's skin as she was undressed, she felt the gentle tickle of breath against her body as layer by layer was removed; finally she stood naked except for the blindfold, her stockings and heels. The nails ran across her stomach and China let out a small sigh, her nipples rose and became sensitive again, her Master's voice shook her back from the bliss of the caress.

"Head up, back straight, arms in the small of your back." She instantly followed his instructions, seconds later he was gently fastening a collar around her throat.

In total darkness she was then led forward, each unsteady step was hard and once or twice she almost stumbled. She felt her Master lift her on one side and on the other nails dug sharply into her soft flesh.

Finally they stopped and China was turned around, her legs were gently pushed back until they met a hard wall.

"Lift your arms above your head." China did as she was told, her bare back pressed against cold metal and she shivered.

Her wrists were suddenly encased in leather, instinctively she pulled down but couldn't move; her ankles were then locked and then a leather belt was placed around her waist. She felt it pull on both sides and panicked a little, unsure of what was about to happen.

"Relax," he told her, she felt mixed up and confused, she trusted him but she didn't know why.

With a lurch she fell backwards, the straps around her wrists and ankles held her body, the strap around her waist ensured she didn't sag in the middle. China felt sick, she almost begged for the blindfold to be removed and then thought better of it, maybe it would be better not to see what was about to happen she told herself.

For long moments she hung motionless, something moved up her leg and her nerves stood on end; the room wasn't cold but she shook anyway. Suddenly her mind cleared – it was a feather she reasoned as it fanned out and teased her skin, China relaxed and enjoyed the thrill.

Despite giving herself over to the sensations overwhelming her, China was careful not to lose control and allow the climax to take her, it was an effort but she dare not unless Master punished her.

Her entire body felt alive, the charges of electricity that surged over her body were so intense, every single part of her skin felt like it was being stroked.

"You may continue." China suddenly felt herself rise up; there was a metallic click when the frame was locked in place. Her ankles and then wrists were untied, her waist belt unfastened and she was guided down onto the floor before the blindfold was removed. Master J stood looking at her, another woman waited for instructions by her side.

"Dress her and then bring her into the main room," he ordered. The woman took China's hand and led her to the stool.

As she sat her hair was pulled back just like the first time she had given herself, only this time she did not prepare herself – the other woman did everything for her. Her hair was drawn back away from her eyes and clipped back, the makeup applied with such care and expertise that China knew the woman was not a novice, she wondered if her dresser had been trained by Master J and a pang of jealousy ran through her body.

The woman turned her on the chair and lifted China's heavy breasts, she gave out a slight moan as the woman circled her nipples with the tips of her thumbs and then expertly circled her areola with the highlighter pencil before painting them red with the lipstick. The transformation was almost complete but China blushed as a finishing touch was applied; the woman ran the tip of the lipstick along the edge of her labia.

"Stand, turn and bend at the waist, place your hands on your knees – push your buttocks up," the woman instructed. China did as she was told, her breasts hanging forward, instinctively she opened her legs to what she felt was the right distance and was aware that the woman could see everything.

The woman bent down and took the pencil, on the right cheek she carefully wrote a large 'X', through which she placed a J.

"Stand." China did as she was told and watched in wonder as a Basque was pulled tight around her body – the lace was drawn up and she felt her breath being stolen. Next stockings were slipped over her toes and pulled smoothly up, she thought her companions fingers lingered a little longer than necessary at the tops of her thighs but relaxed and enjoyed the precious seconds before court shoes were placed in front of her and she stepped into them.

"Look into the mirror." China turned and took in her reflection in the full-length mirror. She looked stunning, every part of her being was larger than life, her eyes darted between her legs and she took in neat triangle of flesh before it disappeared between her closed thighs.

"How do you feel?"

China tried to find the words to describe how she felt – "Overwhelmed."

"You'd better be ready… put on your collar, stand correctly and then enter the other room. I will warn you not to let Master J down, you will be punished in front of his peers should disgrace yourself."

China nodded and walked to the door, she felt the desire to express her gratitude to the other woman and stopped, she turned quickly and kissed the woman on the lips, smiling as she pulled away and straightened up.

The room was full; Domes and subs stood or sat in groups but as a whole they stopped to look at her when China made her entrance. She felt the heat rising in her cheeks as she felt them judge her, some she recognised from before, most were strangers. J stood by the fireplace and she walked towards him, once by his side she dropped her head slightly and relaxed, the room gently buzzed with conversation and China wondered why she was being ignored. She had guessed that her Master wanted to show her off, to teach her something new, instead she was being ignored and she hated it. "China, in the kitchen you will find a tumbler with my vodka in it." J stated and for a moment she wondered why he had mentioned it until realisation dawned and she followed other submissive's through some large double doors.

The room was brightly light and the air clean and fresh unlike the cigarette smoke filled room she had just left; walking to the sink she put her hands down and lent forward, the Basque had been pulled so tight that she felt a little dizzy.

"I haven't seen you before." China spun round to see a clean faced submissive whose blonde hair fell down onto her pale shoulders – she was smaller than China and very attractive, desire stirred deep inside the novice.

"Oh, no, I'm being trained by J," China explained. The girl's eyes widened for a second and she ran water from the tap and took a drink. China watched as the long finger scooped the water into her lips, the newcomer turned her head slightly to look at her.

"I'm Sue. I'm here with my Master." She stood up next to China and leaned against the sink; Sue pressed her buttocks against the cold metal and sighed, "My cheeks are still sore from my training this morning."

"I… I'm China," she held out her hand to the other woman and was startled by the laugh the other woman let out.

"What's your real name?"

"That is her real name," both women jumped as J entered. "I don't like to be kept waiting China, you will learn that."

Sue started to walk towards the door but was stopped by J. "I shall discuss your behaviour with your Master later, see if we can find a suitable punishment." China picked up the glass on the side and walked towards her Master, her hand shook slightly, "It was my fault Master."

"You may leave, Sue," she scuttled from the room as J walked towards China, the tips of his fingers lifted her chin and he looked deeply into her eyes. "Loyalty is one thing, bending the truth to cover for another sub's indiscretion is another. Sue will easily lead you astray if you allow her to." China nodded slowly and held up his drink, J ran his fingers down the side of her face.

"I understand... she is very beautiful," J smiled for a second.

"But you are the one they are talking about; you have a natural pose and presence. I have already been asked who I am training you for."

China looked horrified, "But I don't want to be trained for somebody else, I want to serve you." Her Master walked to the sink and looked out across the rooftops; he drank the remainder of his drink and turned to face her.

"I cannot keep you, I want to but it is not possible. I will train you and then find you a Master that deserves a prize such as yourself."

"I don't want anybody else, Master. I came to serve you – nobody makes me feel this way... How dare you pass me off when you get bored with me?" tears formed in her eyes and she choked on her words.

"How dare you speak to me in such a way, respect and obedience at all times." J rounded on his submissive, his eyes appeared to have sunk into his pale face.

"You should have been honest with me," she countered. J stood trembling before her and China thought for a second he was going to break down, but instead he walked slowly away before pausing for a second. He didn't turn around as he spoke; and the words chilled her to the bone.

"Honesty… Yes, I am dying Sweet China. Even if I could keep you until the end it would not be fair… Ask me for your release."

The words stuck in China's throat, "You Bastard, you started something you couldn't finish and didn't have the nerve to tell me."

"ASK FOR YOUR RELEASE."

"No, you can't push me away now I need to learn more, I need it all."

J seemed to be on automatic pilot, emotions had been unleashed and then shut down in an instant, his refusal to turn and look at her made it worse for China.

"Very well, you have your release." He stood up straight and left her alone in the room.

As China stood on her own time seemed to stop; she barely noticed Sue guiding her into a side room and undressing her. As the basque was removed she looked into China's face, "I'm taking you back to your car, take my number and if there is anything you need call me." China nodded slowly. "Gill I need you to help me get you dressed."

At the sound of her name Gill started to cry uncontrollably. Trembling she pulled on her clothes as Sue cleaned her face.

"My name is China," she sobbed; Sue held her close, stroking her face as she cuddled her.

"I know, but you are not China anymore, you are Gill," Sue explained as she helped her companion to her feet and guided her down to the lift.

At the bottom they stopped as Gill looked up.

"This is a test; he wants to see what I will do."

"No, this is not a test, Gill. You have to get into the car and tell me where you are parked."

EIGHT

Sitting in the garden, the sun browning her shoulders and face China felt a chill wash through her. She looked down between her legs, she had been sitting on a small bank, the grass tickled her feet and it felt like somebody blowing on them. Turning away for a second she wondered if she was losing her mind; when she looked down again J lay there, his head resting on her knees.

"I loved days like this; it would have been good to spend lazy days with you."

China ran her finger through his hair and bent forward to kiss his forehead, it felt cold but she smiled anyway.

"We didn't have enough time together," she sighed before laying back and placing one hand behind her head. "Am I going crazy, is that why I keep seeing you?"

"You are tired, I am a figment of your imagination and you can't let go just yet. You don't feel as ready as you are to move on," J explained, his arms reaching up and his fingers running down the outside of her thighs.

"You are being kind, but if being crazy means I get to keep you then I will accept that."

"But you can't, I will fade and become just a memory but you will go on and live the life you were supposed to lead."

"Will you always be here for me?"

"Haven't I always?!"

China rolled over and bared her cheeks to allow her skin to brown, she reached back and stroked her tattoo, the tip of her nail ran along to letters and she smiled, "eventually, yes."

The Munch was as busy as usual, Gill sat in the centre of the table and joined in all the conversations, her conservative dress and understated appearance hide the submissive inside.

People came and went from the group but she didn't pay most any attention, suddenly a face burst through the crowd and she recognised Sue straight away.

"Hey, Baby." She felt herself being hugged and then kissed on both cheeks.

"What are you doing here? It is so good to see you," Gill gushed; she looked into Sue's face for answers.

"I was in the area and there was somebody I wanted you to meet – I take it you still don't have a Master."

Gill looked down at the table, the others were enveloped in their own conversations and didn't see the sadness wash over her face.

"Come with me." Sue took her hand and led her towards the bar, a well-dressed man waited patiently to be served, Sue ran her hand down his back and patted his bum.

"Anthony, this is Gill. The submissive I told you about," he shuffled round to looked her up and down, she felt his eyes roam all over her for a minute and she felt he seemed a little disappointed in her.

"Hi," his response was cool, it annoyed Sue a little and she shook her head, pulling him down so she could whisper in his ear. Standing up he looked down at her again, this time he took a greater interested in her.

"Can I buy you a drink, Gill?"

"No thanks, I have one."

"She'll have Champagne." Sue gleefully exclaimed before dragging Gill off to the toilet.

"His name is Anthony, he is a friend of my Master's and he is without a submissive at the moment. He is an estate agent, very rich and divorced. He seems to know what he is doing but I have never been around him in the scene. Master says he is just what you need," Sue chattered as soon as the door closed.

"Have you seen J?" Gill asked, she took a lipstick out and refreshed her lips, using the mirror to watch Sue's expression.

"No and neither has anybody else. Forget him, he was overrated anyway."

"You never spent time with him… or did you?" Gill ran her fingers over Sue's stomach, stroking in small circles. She watched her friend squirm under the caress, Sue had never hidden the fact she wanted to fuck Gill but her Master did not allow it. This didn't stop Gill tormenting her friend at every given opportunity.

"No, God I want you," Sue breathed through clenched teeth, her nipples erect and clearly visible through her black mesh top; her legs parted slightly and she could almost have been sweating.

"Tell me more about Anthony," Gill pushed. She found him attractive but refused to be sucked into another bad experience.

Sue pushed against the flat of her hand and mentally willed it to go lower, "He's been single for about a year, I think he has been a Dom for five years but I'm not sure so don't quote me on that."

Gill removed her hand and kissed Sue tenderly, "Thanks, I'll see what he has to say for himself."

The bar was already emptying when they emerged, Anthony waited in the corner with a bottle and a couple of glasses, as soon as they sat down Sue's mobile rang.

"Ok, I'm on my way," she stood up again and looked down at the others as she snapped it shut, "I'm really sorry to do this to you but I have to go, I'll leave my phone if you need me… have fun."

They watched her rushing out the door and then sat in an uneasy silence for a moment.

"Was that planned, do you think?" Gill asked; Anthony grinned at her.

"Knowing her Master, no, he has a habit of being totally clumsy and incapable of anything. I think we both know who wears the trousers in their relationship really." He poured her a glass of Champagne and sat back to watch her drink.

"I understand that you have been in the scene for a while," she asked directly, preferring to get the basics over and done with.

"I know my way around a dungeon, you?"

Gill was a little startled at his terminology, "Maybe I am not what you are looking for, Sir."

"I think you will find I am very accommodating," he stated, "I am very easy to get along with."

The morning light woke Gill, she turned over in the bed and looked at Anthony, his features were handsome; He opened his eyes and smiled at her, running his fingers down her side.

"I will take breakfast in the conservatory; you will remain naked until such time as I collar you." The words caught Gill by surprise. She rose and showered and feeling a little self conscious she wandered into the kitchen and prepared tea, toast and cereal which she arranged neatly on a tray before walking through the house to the conservatory at the back of the house.

Anthony waited, on the chair by his side was a leather-riding crop, on the table sat a leather collar with a single stud in the centre and a ring to one side. Gill remembered the plain one J had made her wear; it was simple like him, unobtrusive.

Placing the tray on the table she offered each item to Anthony and then stood waiting for his next instruction. She watched him pour the tea, his eyes briefly inspected her but he said nothing, instead his fingers toyed with the collar. Gill wanted him to speak, she wanted to feel the collar around her soft neck – the comfort it brought would make the agony of the silence worthwhile.

"Kneel and crawl to me." Gill did as he requested, crawling over the hard stone which hurt her knees. "Now you may suck my cock."

She slowly pulled his zip down, running her fingers over his smooth cock; it grew steadily in her hand before she took it in her mouth. There was a faint smell of stale urine and she wanted to choke, pulling back slightly until he gripped her hair and stopped her.

"You will learn to do exactly as you are told or you will feel the punishment for not doing so." Roughly he fucked her mouth, Gill's fingers gripped his trousers tightly and she tried desperately to give herself the opportunity to breathe.

Within minutes he had climaxed; the salty sperm filled her mouth and ran down her chin – Anthony grunted and released his grip, his limp cock slipped from her mouth and rested against her chin. Reaching forward he took the collar and slipped it around her neck, pulling it tight and almost choking her. There was a faint snap and Gill realised that the collar was locked in place.

"Clean my cock and then go and wash your face," his vulgarity confused Gill a little and she knelt motionless for a moment unsure what to do next, finally she took a napkin from the table and cleaned his organ, running the soft cotton under his foreskin before retreating back inside the house.

China spent the entire day in the garden avoiding the hustle of the house, a dinner party was planned and she thought it best to keep out of the way. Caterers filled the kitchens and when she went in for lunch she felt she got in the way. China noticed as well that the novice stayed out of her way, she wondered briefly if she had overstepped herself but then put it into the back of her mind, the girl had to learn she reasoned.

Finally in the early evening torches were lit in the garden along one of the paths and guests started to arrive, they passed the house and were escorted down to a marquee that had been arranged in the garden.

China had spent the latter half of the afternoon bathing and arranging her clothes, now as she stepped from the French windows that led into her room she was aware of the looks she was receiving. Instead of the sombre black everyone expected her to wear she had opted for a deep blue dress that lifted her breasts and extenuated her curves, her stiletto heels clicked sharply on the path as she walked unescorted down to the guests, her Master's collar remained in place around her throat.

Most of the guests she recognised from one event or another, and at the end of the path stood Anthony; he was immaculately dressed and at his feet knelt his sub. China recognised her immediately but refused to acknowledge the fact – she gave Anthony a slight smile and curled her top lip a little as a warning. It was primeval and unnecessary but she enjoyed watching him turn away.

"Ladies and Gentlemen, Honoured guests. Welcome to my home," the master of the house announced as the doors to the marquee opened and a sumptuous table was revealed. The master motioned for China to enter; as the guest of honour she was escorted to the head of the table and sat next to the host, people openly stared, others talked in hushed whispers as they were waited on and the wine flowed freely.

China watched as naked women walked down both sides of the table, stopping at set places. Although they were different shapes and sizes all wore the same masks and each stood wavering in high heeled shoes. Finally, a smaller, petit woman was lifted onto the table; she walked slowly and methodically down the centre between the dishes, her breasts swaying with each step. Some guests ignored her, others unaccustomed to such sights sat open mouthed.

Eventually she reached the very centre of the table and knelt down in a space that had been cleared, the woman lifted her head slightly, her legs spread wide. China could see her nipples were swollen and hard. A male sub, one of the few at the gathering, poured champagne for everyone and when he finished he leaned across the table and slipped the remaining bottle between the kneeling slave's legs – she let out a gasp of pleasure as the bottle neck slipped between her lips and deep into her sex, the base of the bottle rested at an angle on the table and she remained motionless.

"Did your Master ever show you such extravagance?" China's host asked, leaning close so the others could not hear.

"My Master was more refined." She replied, holding the glass to her red lips and taking gentle sip, refusing to be moved by his comments.

"Is there no man at this table you would call 'Master'?" he pushed.

"Do you mean, Anthony? I am sure he has impressed you with his tales of topping me," China challenged. Anthony looked up from his conversation and smiled.

"Do I hear my exploits being discussed?" he asked grinning broadly. China rose gently to her feet and stood behind him; her long nails running across his cheek.

"Anthony is a really powerful Master… He takes emotionally crippled women and humiliates them." China gripped the base of his hair and pulled him up. The smirk wiped from his face, all control slipping away, "In order to get my submission he humiliated and beat me after seducing me…"

He choked on the little food in his mouth and tried desperately to break free from her grip; China strengthened her hold and pulled him further back into his chair. Slowly she leaned down so that her lips were close to his ear. Anthony could feel the softness of her breath, the gentle malice that she whispered for his benefit and his benefit alone.

"Do you remember what you did to me? I do… in every detail." His face paled at her words and he loosened the grip on the chain connecting him to the sub kneeling by his side.

Standing, China smiled, raised her glass and called for a toast to their host.

NINE

Gill stood and looked out of the window from Anthony's bedroom, as was his instructions she was not allowed to wear clothes from the moment she arrived until the moment she left him. Her new master allowed his friends and guests gaze at her, she knew they wanted her but he took great delight in teasing her in front of them, forcing her to degrade herself in front of them.

She tried to break free from his will but she was drawn back like a moth to a flame, her thoughts were constantly of J, she wondered if this would have been her fate if he had kept her. With her mind in turmoil the only thing she could hold onto were the commands Anthony issued her, no matter how hard they were. The only thing she refused was to respond to was the name J had given her. It drove Anthony mad that she would not bend on the issue but he bided his time to exact the right degree of punishment.

After a month Gill was lost, she stood numbly as dinner was served, the serving staff had moving around her as though she were not there. Naked except for her collar Gill stood next to her master, he had watched her shave between her legs to ensure that she was displayed fully. When the guests arrived she knelt between his legs, pushing her breasts out and spreading her legs. Anthony wasted no time in telling them she would do anything they asked – they could fuck her if they wished. Some smiled at his attitude but she could tell by their expressions that they humoured him and underneath the real Dom's considered him crass and uncouth.

A large fat man stopped in front of them, Gill recognised him as one of J's associates and she wondered if he would come. The man tenderly lifted her chin in the palm of his hand and winked at her, his other hand dropped slightly and he tweaked her nipples hard enough to make her feel uncomfortable.

Eventually all the guests had arrived and dinner began, conversation was light and Gill drifted in and out of her thoughts, she was aware that the fat man was watching her, his eyes never left her face. Anthony too had noticed and he leaned across to her, "Tonight you will give yourself to him."

She stood, shocked at the order; she nodded blushing. Anthony stood, his proud features became the centre of everyone's attention, an uneasy hush settled over the room.

"I wish to thank you all for coming, drinks will be served in the play room." A slight murmur ran around the table, "I thought you all might like to be present when Gill tastes severe punishment for the first time."

The walls to the playroom were lined with dark cork, it was the first time Gill had been allowed in and it scared her. Large metal pulleys dangled menacingly from beams running across the ceiling and hidden spotlights cast small circles of light on silver and black pieces of equipment.

"Stand in the centre of the room, hands behind your back." Anthony instructed. Gill did as she was told but shook visibly.

Roughly he locked leather wrist restraints in place, pulling back hard on her hair to make her look straight ahead. "Legs apart – wider." Gill felt cold metal lock around her ankles, then her knees. She chanced a look down and saw a silver restraining bar; her stomach was tightening in a knot of nerves as she was left unsure of what was planned for her.

"Who controls you?" Anthony's voice was close to her ear although he did not whisper his question as J had.

"You do Master." Her throat was dry and beads of sweat formed on her forehead, goose-bumps rose on her flesh and she trembled harder. She was aware that her nipples were hardening and that her sex was wet. No sound came from the guests watching in the darkness.

"Tell me your name?" he asked, Gill was aware that some, if not all the guests knew that J had given her the name 'China'.

"Gill." She stammered, fear was setting in but she remained defiant.

"Tell me your proper name."

"Gill…" her arms were pulled up her back suddenly, pain shot through her shoulders as her arms were stretched up to the ceiling.

"Tell me your REAL NAME." Anthony hissed the question through clenched teeth; Gill was aware that she was humiliating him in front of the others, "or would you prefer to suffer the consequences?"

"My name is Gill. That is my given name, Master."

The first biting stroke ripped into her flesh, the skin on her buttocks rising in a welt that flashed red and then white. She was aware of the scream that emerged from her lips, but forced herself to bite the corner of her mouth to control the pain. She pulled her head back, pulling against wrist straps.

"Master please… NO," the second stroke didn't feel as hard as the first but numbness was already setting in and Gill braced herself against it.

"I know now why your last Master dumped you." The venom in his voice was almost worse than the blows he rained down on her soft skin, "You don't know how to follow orders and you don't deserve to be owned."

Tears started to roll down her cheeks, his words burned deep down inside and made her wonder if he was correct. She was trying to count the strikes and reckoned that she had taken five when he stopped suddenly, the entire room suddenly became still.

"Give her some water," a voice in the darkness instructed, Anthony walked in front of her, Gill's head had fallen forward and she fought hard to remain conscious.

"Do you want water Whore?" He held a glass to her lips but didn't tip it for her to be able to drink.

"Please, please."

"Tell me your name… Say China and I will let you down."

"But my name is Gill!" Anthony tipped the glass up, water covered her face, flooded her mouth and spilled down her body. She drank greedily, gulping the precious liquid down as fast as she could. For the first time she could see the cane he had used on her cheeks, it was a shorter than she imagined but quickly turned her attention back to her Master. She looked him in the eye, "Gil.."

He turned away, placing the cane on a small table. His fingers toyed with a ball gag; he watched the horror of realisation creep across her face and walked towards her.

"If you won't say your name then you will say nothing." He gripped her chin and forced open her mouth so that he could ease the gag into her mouth. She fought with every fibre of her will, desperately pushing the ball with her tongue as he tied it behind her head. Her eyes fixed on him whenever he came into view, desperate to see what he planned next.

Anthony fixed his gaze on the wall behind her, a vast array of crops, canes and whips hung by their handles from brass hooks, his fingers ran across leather and wood; on a small shelf underneath he spied nipple clamps, a smile stretched across his lips.

The clamps squeezed Gill's nipples hard as Anthony slowly tightened the screws; a single silver chain pulled her heavy breasts together. The gag muffled her cries; her breathing was laboured past the obstruction and through her nose.

"I own you, do you understand?" he mocked. Gill nodded, her eyes slightly glazed by pain. Anthony took a silver chain and clipped it onto her collar, he passed it down between her breasts, attaching it to the nipple chain and down through her legs, he passed it along her labia and up between her burning buttocks. Slowly he pulled a leather belt tight around her waist and then clipped the chain to it.

As she breathed the tiny links of metal rubbed her clitoris, electricity flowed through every nerve in her body, it seemed almost too subtle for Anthony, he seemed to be more direct, brutal.

"A little something I borrowed from your former Master." Gill whimpered a little at the memory of the touch, the burning desire inside her for his protection and not those belonging to this impostor. Finally a silk scarf was placed across her eyes; she stopped fighting him, too weary to do anything but accept his punishment.

As her breasts rose and fell with her breathing Gill was aware of every sound in the room. Her senses were heightened by the blindfold but gave her a false indication of everything going on around her. She could taste and smell the air, it seemed to be sweet and full of the scent of sex and sweat; whispering people remained just out of full earshot.

The first blow to cross her breasts stung with a thousand pin pricks; her back arched and she tried to pull away from the smacks, at first they covered her stomach and chest, then the tops of her legs and finally her back and buttocks. She tried to scream but found her voice muffled by the gag - every inch of her skin felt like it was being torn from her bones, then everything stopped. As she sobbed uncontrollably burning cold was pressed into her tender stomach, Gill felt her bladder contract and she wet herself.

The warm urine ran down her legs and onto the floor, she desperately tried to stop it; humiliation tore her apart and she felt violated. For the first time she felt the wrist straps cutting into her arms as they bore her full weight. When she stopped Anthony released her.

Unable to stand he made her kneel on the floor, legs apart, as he took off the blindfold and turned on the lights. Like an animal she crawled through her own mess, the torment of the metal chain continued as he walked her like a dog around the guests so they could look at her.

"Who wants her now?" he stated. Occasionally he would turn her with the end of the cane so they could all see his handiwork.

"I will take her tonight." Gill looked up into the face of a blonde Domme, her face seemed familiar but Gill couldn't concentrate through the pain.

"Very well, she is yours for the night. If she fails to please you then tell me in the morning and little Miss Gill will find her punishment doubled." Anthony handed the leash to the woman and led his guests out of the room. She squatted down, her fingers unbuckling the gag, lifting Gill's chin with a nailed finger.

"It's time you took your release and returned to your real Master. What is your name?" her voice was soft and tender.

"China, my name is China." Gill broke, tears fell like raindrops down her flushed cheeks and she buried herself in the Domme's embrace, the woman's fingers ran through her hair and felt a small comfort.

The bedroom door closed and China lent against it, her hands covered her sex, she tried so hard not to look the other woman in the eyes.

"Go into the bathroom and run a hot bath, I'll be there in a moment." She followed the instructions, watching the water rise in the enamel bath rather than daring to look round. Every sound made her jump, every touch of cold air made her tremble until finally she was sure the Domme was behind her.

Tenderly the hair was pulled back away from China's face and tied back, the release of her collar was followed by the chains and belt – excitement filled her as the woman wrapped her arms around her body and unscrewed the nipple clamps. Slowly feeling returned to China's nipples; long nails raked her skin and a single kiss was placed on the sub's shoulder. China turned and looked into the woman's eyes.

"You remember me?" China saw straight away that she was girl who had been with J the first time she had met him; she nodded, "If it were possible would you return to your true Master?"

China nodded. "You must ask for your release in the morning, climb into the bath and let's clean you up."

As China slipped into the hot water tiredness overtook her and she closed her eyes, nimble fingers massaged her aching body and gave her release from the painful knots of nerves.

She became aware at one point that the fat man entered the room and held a brief conversation with her Domme, too tired to care she reasoned that she must have dreamt it and closed her eyes again until the water turned cold and she was roused.

The softness of the bed seemed to swallow her, China wanted so much to fall asleep and forget the pain of the night's events. Through half closed eyes she turned her head and looked into the face of the Domme by her side.

"You have been given instructions, I expect you to follow them," the woman whispered, a smile crossed her lips and China wanted so much to kiss them. She rolled slightly and allowed herself to be guided to the woman's exposed nipple she flicked her tongue around the areola and pulled it gently between her teeth. The Domme let out a small groan and fell back into the bed. China looked deep into her eyes as she suckled greedily from both nipples in turn – her fingers slipped slowly up the inside of the Domme's thigh and for the first time she found herself running her index finger along other woman's lips. At first she was surprised at the wetness, then as her confidence grew at the pleasure she was installing in her partner China started to circle the woman's clitoris before pressing gently with two fingers.

"May I taste you, Mistress?" China asked desperate for permission as the Mistress raised her hips to China's touch.

"You may," she purred. China removed her fingers from the woman's groin and raised them to her lips to suck.

"Not like that pretty, honey should only be tasted with the tongue to keep its purity." China blushed at the statement but slipped down between the Domme's legs, kissing her pubic mound gently. She continued to blush as the woman guided her head to the right spot, gripping China's head she pushed up and instinctively China nuzzled and then licked, her mouth closed around the woman's tiny button and she sucked softly.

"Jesus, yes," chancing a glance China looked up, the woman was gripping the bed covers, beads of sweat appeared on her forehead and her face was a picture of pleasure. She bit her lip as China returned to the task at hand, first sucking gently and then pushing her tongue deep inside the other woman; she tasted the sweet nectar and found herself eager to make Mistress want more. Without warning a climax ripped though her body as she rubbed herself against the covers, fucking an invisible partner as she strove to give pleasure as ordered by Master Anthony.

The woman's fingers dug into her hair and then relaxed as her own climax subsided, she laughed gently and her breasts trembled, "I think your Master will find it very difficult to let you go."

"Will he? I don't think he will, I do not please him," China whispered, her head rested on the Domme's thigh.

"Anthony will let you go, but he will hate doing it. He is nothing but a lout and a second rate Master. I think you drove him nuts tonight by not giving in, but who can blame you?" She continued to stroke China's hair tenderly, "This is not where you belong."

TEN

China woke early and prepared her Mistresses clothes before stealing out the door and going down to the kitchen, stopping to look at the bruises and lash marks that covered her beautiful body.

The redness of the wrist strap burns had not diminished and she mentally cursed Anthony for the humiliation he had put her through – she felt it was uncalled for and prayed he would give her the release she intended to request.

When she stepped into the kitchen he was sitting with his back to her, she leaned against the frame and took a deep breath, bowed her head and walked to his side.

"Did you do as you were told?" he asked and China nodded. "Good, now you can take care of my cock, it is still covered in the cunt juices of the slave who benefited from it after you left."

He gripped her hair and pushed his hardening cock into the back of her mouth, filling her throat with the tip and causing her to choke. He laughed at her attempts to push back.

"Take it like the greedy little bitch you are." She managed to pull her head back and started to suck the length of his shaft, flicking her tongue around the end and pushed it under his foreskin. His grip relaxed as he started to breathe deeply, her soft mouth working expertly at his manhood. As usual he climaxed within minutes, holding her just long enough to allow his semen to disappear down her throat before pulling out.

China knelt stunned between his legs for a minute and then rose to her feet.

"Master, I wish to ask something of you." She looked into his face as it grew red with anger.

"You dare to ask for something!"

"I wish my release. Today."

Anthony seemed lost for words – his eyes narrowed and finally rage managed to escape his lips, "Why? Is it that Domme you spent last night with? Do you think she will treat you any better than I?"

"Please, Master. I appreciate everything you have done for me, but this is not what I want, what I need and I would hate to disappoint you," China changed tone and tried to make it sound as though she felt as though she would let him down in time.

"I have never had a sub ask for release…"

"There is a first time for everything, Anthony." China looked up at the door, her Mistress leaned against the wood and fixed her stare on Anthony, "We all lose subs, its time for her to move on, to find herself."

"You did this." He accused, "You turned her against me."

"No Anthony, you did that yourself with your heavy hand and your inexperience." She motioned China forward, "Get your possessions it's time we left, my car is outside."

The front door looked so inviting as China walked towards it. She had slipped on her only possessions, the two things Anthony allowed her to bring, her coat and shoes. The Mistress waited patiently as China stepped through the door and into the back of the car; the sub's breasts rubbed the inside of her coat and she had to tell herself that this was not the time.

"You ungrateful Bitch. You came to me with nothing, you leave with nothing and I hope I never lay eyes on you again," Anthony's face was bright red and he glowered at her through the open car door.

"Thank you for everything, Anthony. I would like to leave you with something." China maintained her composure, "My name is China, thank you for helping me find myself."

66

The door closed and they pulled away, China smiled to herself and stretched out on the back seat, she was going to find her Master, she was going to make him want her, she was going to make him need her, to love her.

She was going home.

The night remained cool; China walked through the grounds and sat on a bench by the pond. Leaning forward she ran her hands through the icy water and smiled to herself – she may have cast a fly in the ointment at the dinner but it was worth it, the look on Anthony's face alone was worth any punishment the master of the house levelled at her.

"Happy?" a warm kiss brushed her bare should and she closed her eyes.

"Yes. Master am I being a Domme?" She tingled deep inside, shaking her hair free.

"No, you have learnt not to suffer fools gladly. I am very proud of you, of what you have become." J's voice surrounded her, filling her mind with its gentleness.

"I think I understand, will I find a Master to guide me."

"Yes, he may never replace me but he will not expect to."

"I will never forget you," she whispered.

Another kiss brushed her shoulder and he was gone again.

The door to the flat pushed open slowly and China stepped into the hall; in the distance behind another closed door she could hear music. She slipped off her coat and walked steadily forward, her hand hovered slightly before she knocked.

"Enter," his voice sounded shallow and for a moment China wondered if it was J waiting in the room on the other side.

She held her head up and turned the handle, with her chest pushed out and with a confident stride she walked through to face him. The shock that greeted her was almost too much and China fought her first impulse to turn away.

"Yes?" J sounded a little confused as he focused on her.

"Master J, it's China, I have come back to learn from you, to serve you, to give myself to you." She stated confidently. She was sure she could smell alcohol in the air; pills lay scattered across the table. His hands shook slightly and he couldn't look at her for long before his head dropped slightly.

"Turn around sweet China, show me what you have endured."

China turned slowly around, his eyes searched every inch of her flailed skin, "That was not necessary. Come kneel before me."

Eager she did as she was told, her head bowed almost in his lap, gently he stroked her hair.

"I am sorry I am not properly prepared for you Master, I will do so when you allow me to." J lifted her face in his hands and brushed her lips with his. Deep in her chest her heart pounded, she caught her breath as he kissed her with a passion she had forgotten. It was the kind of kiss that told her she was alive, wanted, it ran down her spine and sent heat surging through her sex, her nipples tingled with excitement. She wanted to please him.

"You may climax," he whispered it directly into her ear, his arm locked under hers to steady her.

"I can't, not this soon Master." China warned, J simply pressed his hand between her legs. She hardly had time to register the touch consciously when the fire inside her exploded.

"Oh myyyyyyyyyyy God." She moaned, it was hard to breath and J's grip around her didn't help.

"When you climax show me respect and say my name," she nodded at the instruction, her eyes had snapped wide apart and she started at him. "How did you…"

"I am inside you, I control you. Not with the cane or crop," his fingers brushed her buttocks, "but with my will and knowledge."

China closed her eyes and buried her head in his shoulder, she felt light headed and drowsy, she barely had time to register his words when another climax erupted deep inside and more intense than the first.

"J," she breathed, he released his grip.

"Master J," he corrected, guiding her head down into his lap, finger stroking her soft cheeks.

China woke in bed, confused she looked around the light filled room. She felt the weight of her Master's body next to her but was afraid to turn in case it was a dream waiting to be shattered. Finally she plucked up the courage and rolled over, his complexion was pale, China watched his chest rise and fall, it was shallow and he seemed to be fighting for every precious breath. She felt fingernails rake up her thigh and turned suddenly, the Domme that had brought her to him stood by the side of the bed; she placed her finger to her lips to indicate silence and took China's hand. She led her from the bed into the lounge, held her close and kissed her eyes.

"Mistress, why?"

"I am not a Mistress, my name is Teri," she looked deep into China's eyes before turning her to face the bedroom, "J is dying, did he tell you?"

China nodded her head, "Yes, but I would have guessed."

"You have a choice little bird, stay and allow him to teach you while he is able. Or…"

"Or leave and never feel as whole as I do now."

Teri wrapped her arms around China's torso, her nails dug in slightly and made small circles on China's skin.

"Will you be alright?" China reached back, her head rested on the other woman's shoulder.

"I think so."

"May I give you a piece of advice?" China turned her head to look at the woman and nodded, "Do not fall in love with him."

"It's too late for that, I think I already am."

ELEVEN

China laid out J's clothes on the bed and watched him shave, his hand shook slightly and she noticed he had cut himself. Gently she took the razor from his hand and standing behind him she carefully glided the blade over his face, his eyes remained focused on her actions.

When she finished he patted his face with a towel and wandered into the bedroom, he pulled on his clothes and opened a drawer.

"Come to me and sit on the edge of the bed." China moved quickly, her naked body rippled with anticipation. Once she had taken her position he lifted her hair and slipped her old leather collar into place, China dropped her head slightly and blushed.

"Thank you, Master," she whispered hoarsely.

His hand ran up her thigh and his thumb tickled the soft skin between her thigh and groin, she sucked in a lungful of air and sat bolt upright.

"We are going shopping today. Put on the long coat you will find in the hall and your shoes, nothing else."

"Master, may I say something," his eyes searched her for a second.

"Yes."

"I want to tell you how glad I am here with you, that you took me back." When she had finished China stood and carried out his instructions before waiting patiently by the door.

J emerged fully dressed, his white shirt tucked loosely into his trousers, shoes polished and a light jacket pulled over his broad shoulders, China felt exposed compared to her Master.

China drove them into town, J's hand rested on her naked thigh but she was not sure where he was looking, he covered his eyes with the blackest sunglasses she had ever seen, they gave his face a sinister expression that sent a chill down her spine. When they parked and walked she became aware that people looked at J, not her and she relaxed, completely naked seemed natural to her.

As they walked passed all the clothes stores China couldn't help but wonder where he was taking her; they turned a corner into a side street and she was led into a doorway so small that J was forced to bend slightly. Inside the walls were covered in flock wallpaper, two high backed chairs sat in the middle of the room, the centrepiece was a slightly raised plinth. "China, take off your coat and step onto the platform," J ordered. Uneasily she did as she was told, the cold air of the shop making her flesh rise in small goose-bumps; her nipples hardened automatically and she turned in time to see J flick the catch down on the door.

"Sir, so good to see you again," the voice came from behind her and China spun round to see the owner. An elegant woman dressed in a very ornate leather catsuit had entered from the back and strode purposely across wooden floor, "You have brought me a new customer, perhaps one of your clients' little toys?"

China tried to place the accent but settled for European, possibly French. The woman's make-up was thick, her lips painted black with a touch of purple, she perched on six inch heels, her small bust displayed through narrow slits in the top.

She turned and ran a long nail up China's thigh, digging it in just enough to leave a scratch, "She is more fully figured than the rest, slightly older..."

"China is my sub," the words stopped the woman in her track, "Madam Sophia, take extra care of her for me."

She clapped her hands and two young girls emerged from the back, their bodies were packed into tight rubber outfits that appeared to have been painted onto their bodies, China could see each had a matching nipple ring in her left nipple, small chains dangled from them.

"Deep purple I think, have you any instructions, Sir?" Madame asked. J flicked his finger at her and motioned her forward, when he finished whispering a broad grin stretched across the woman's face.

"Certainly Sir, for you anything." She crossed the room to China and pulled a piece of cloth from a tiny cupboard in the wall which she wrapped across China's eyes, telling her to relax.

For over an hour hands touched and measured her body, pulled and eased China in various directions, clothes touched her skin, were pulled tight and then removed. Once or twice her skin became cold as a liquid was applied and then peeled off, her nerves felt on fire. When the blindfold was finally removed China looked at herself in the full-length mirror the two subs held up; she tried to breath, she looked amazing. She had been pulled into a leather bodice that lifted her breasts, they had been pulled together to make a tight cleavage but it wasn't an uncomfortable feeling. Her eyes flicked over the lines and she could make out oriental scripture stitched into the surface.

The skirt was tight at the top and flared toward the bottom, two slits allowed her legs to move easily and at the back a small flap allowed voyeurs to view her buttocks.

Boxes sat piled by the door on a stool. China's eyes widened and she couldn't help but smile as her legs were lifted one by one and her shoes were replaced with stockings and ankle boots.

"Master… thank you." J guided her out the door and she felt on cloud nine as they walked towards the car. In a doorway a girl sat begging and J stopped and bent down, his hand fished into his pocket and he pulled out some change, he slipped it into her hand and turned it, her wrists were burned and scarred, he lifted her chin in his hand and looked into her glazed eyes.

He stood and put his arm around China's waist, kissing the side of her head and guiding her back to the car. Once they were inside J slipped his hand under the coat and ran his fingers along her lips, teasing her clitoris until she found it hard to breath, gripping the steering wheel for support. "Master... please... please may I climax?" she begged, her eyes were closed tight and the corner of her lip was being bitten between her teeth. "Look at me," her eyes blinked open and stared at him, her mouth fell open and China felt her lips swell as the blood rushed to her cheeks and her groin, "you may."

"Ohhhhhhhhh my God." The shakes started in the centre of her body and stretched out until her entire frame trembled and shook forcing her to grip the steering wheel tighter to maintain steady.

TWELVE

The flat seemed a little cold and China ran her fingers along the radiators, they were icy and she quickly turned up the thermostat. The streetlights were already lit and she slipped off her coat and stepped out of her work clothes, as J had instructed she wore her collar as soon as she finished work, only in the house did she transform herself into her true self.

"Master?" she called out into the darkness, it was unusual not to find him sitting at the computer or in the kitchen preparing their evening meal. She padded through the flat wondering where he was until she pushed open the door to the bedroom.

J lay on the bed, his eyes glued shut, his forehead was sweating and he shook violently; quickly China slipped two pills into his mouth and lifted him slightly so that he could swallow before placing him back on the mattress. The covers were drenched and China quickly changed them, wrapping him up in a blanket and cradling his head in her arms until he fell asleep.

She watched him for a few minutes to make sure he was settled before settling down in the study, she dropped into his leather chair and turned on the light by the computer. On a square piece of velvet cloth sat a long silver chain, China recognised it as similar one to the Anthony had put her in, only this one seemed more delicate, the links were small and there didn't seem to be as much as the first one.

"I made it for you," the voice behind her was weak but she didn't turn around to face him, she ran her fingers over the cold metal.

"Thank you, J. It's very beautiful, how do I wear it?"

"You wear it under your work clothes, a little reminder of me," he rested his head on the doorframe for a moment before crossing the room towards her. "Stand up."

China quickly did as she was told, her hands automatically rested in the small of her back and she tried to keep eye contact with J as he slipped the long section of chain around her waist. There was very little weight and China couldn't help but smile as she thought of the heavy one Anthony had locked her into. She looked into the mirror to watch as J threaded the smaller chain between her legs, tiny balls rubbed against her lips for a moment before disappearing between the soft folds. J clipped the end of the chain up at the back, it was cold against the cheeks of her warm buttocks but within seconds China felt comfortable and at ease.

J stood up and looked at her, the palm of his hand rested against her cheek and she nuzzled instinctively.

"Thank you, Master," she whispered, turning her head slightly to kiss his tender palm.

He walked through the flat, China following close behind with her head slightly bowed, but instead of turning into the bedroom J led her into a small room she had never been allowed to enter.

The walls had been lined with dark cork, a frame dominated the centre of the room and China felt herself guided towards it. J locked her wrists into the top; the softest velvet lined leather gripped her.

"Put your feet into the straps at the bottom," J instructed her. China looked down and slipped her feet in the leather loops at the bottom.

From behind her Master wrapped a thin leather strap around her waist, and a thick chain locked her securely onto the metal sides. Finally J slipped a blindfold across her eyes and stroked her mouth.

"Relax, you're quite safe here."

She felt his finger run down her spine, shivers ran the full length of her back and the muscles in her stomach contracted.

"Do you trust me?" he asked.

China merely nodded her head. The frame clicked and vibrated for a second before she fell forward slowly, the frame easily held her weight and China felt her long dark hair fall forward over shoulders.

Ice-cold sensations ran from the nape of her neck, down her spinal cord and along the chain wrapped around her waist before slipping easily down between her buttocks. Without warning drops of heat exploded along the same path, each capsule of molten lava stung intensely as it followed the path of its predecessor. China felt her lips tremble, they were dry and sensitive and she ran her tongue around her mouth to wet them.

As her heavy breasts hung down totally exposed, J ran his fingers around her nipples without touching them, he teased the areola to the point where her entire body strained forward desperately for more. Just when China thought it wouldn't be any worse her Master rolled her nipples between finger and thumb, her swollen nipples became hard under his manipulation.

"Who do you serve?" The words came like a gunshot in the darkness.

"You, Master, always you." China hesitated – she didn't understand why he would ask such as thing when he already knew the answer.

"Who owns you?"

Once again China fought to clear her mind in order to understand the context of the question, "Master J owns me… Mind, body & soul," she stated.

Without warning J pressed his palm between her legs, his index finger pressed her clitoris, the other fingers pulled the delicate silver chain tight against her sex.

"You may climax," he stated. China's wrists and ankles pulled against their restraints, her entire body rocked and shuddered. Even if she had wished to there was nothing that could have stopped the intense climax that erupted deep inside her.

When it rolled away she fought for breath, the frame swung up and China found herself falling the other way until her body was almost horizontal. China hung in the air, time lost all sense of purpose, the room remained perfectly quiet and she started to panic slightly. If J was ill then she might not be able to get out of the frame to help him. She pulled against the wrists straps hard, fighting to free her wrists without success.

As she took a deep breath she was aware of the scent of burning wax, moments later the drops fell onto her breasts and down her cleavage, this time she tried so hard to twist away from the needle like pains. Try as she might it was impossible for China to stop crying out, her head rolled from side to side and she whimpered uncontrollable. Finally the last drop fell and she was left alone as the wax hardened on her skin.

"Are you awake, Sweet China?"

"Yes, Master," she muttered; J slipped between her legs and ran his fingers along her. He bent slightly and blew gently against her labia, the swollen lips parted slightly causing China to suck in air.

"You want to feel me inside you." His submissive remained quiet and J ran his fingers across her stomach pulling at the tiny flecks of wax. "You keep wondering why I have not made love to you, taken you totally."

It seemed to China that he was reading her mind; a million questions flooded her thoughts, without warning the tip of his tongue circled her clitoris sending waves of pleasure surging throughout her body.

"Please Master, may I climax?" She gritted her teeth as she desperately fought the need to do so. Abruptly J stopped and his lips hovered above her pubic mound before he bit the flesh tenderly.

China's mouth opened and her head fell back, slowly at first she felt herself tingle inside and although she fought to control her body it did not respond; she was wetter now than she could have imagined, her breath was taken away as her lips parted and the climax started. As she struggled against the tide of passion her head was lifted and the blindfold removed, her eyes opened and she look up J standing between her legs for the first time.

Her lips moved as she tried to beg, the length of his cock rubbed gently against her lips as he held her head for her to see, when she tried to close her eyes he ordered her to open them. The soundless words soon dried in her throat and China was forced to beg with her eyes, climaxing without permission would mean displeasing her Master, a feeling she hated more than anything.

As the pleasure started to turn to torture J lifted her head a little higher and stopped moving, his eyes caught hers and almost hypnotically he started to talk.

"When you climax you will say my name. Always say my name, understand?"

China lazily moved her head in agreement, her body ran hot and cold, she passed into a haze of euphoria and in an instant she offered him her mind, body and soul. A simple smile crossed J's lips and he stroked her nipples.

"You may climax," her muscles strained against her bonds and she thrashed violently in midair, her groin muscles flexed and rippled, desperate to feel his cock inside them.

"Master J," she hissed before letting out a cry of desire so strong that J was forced to place his hand over her mouth. Without thinking she bit hard, her teeth sinking into his soft flesh and drawing blood.

China lay suspended until she caught back her breath before J pushed the frame upright; he unclipped her legs and wrists before helping her to step free. She had just cleared the metal when China felt her legs give way and before she realised what had happened J picked her up, carried her into the bedroom and laid her tenderly on the bed.

Her eyes felt heavy and closed willingly, she never felt the chain being removed from her waist or saw her Master sitting in the half light watching her sleep.

China walked through the grounds back towards the house; she could hear the sounds of the dinner continuing in the distance and decided to take the long route back to avoid being seen.

As she approached the house a middle-aged man sat on the seat by the door, a panatela cigar nestled between his fingers as he watched her approach.

"Good evening," he said, his eyes met hers and China thought she recognised something familiar.

"Good evening. I'm sorry I don't know you do I?" It was a statement of fact that made the stranger look at her long and hard.

"No, we have never met but you are the main topic of conversation at everybody's dinner table at the moment."

China's face blushed at the words; she turned to look back at the marquee, "I don't know why, I haven't done anything out of the ordinary."

"Do not underestimate yourself, the woman who had an effect on Master J and who carry's his mark no less," once again China felt herself blushing at the words.

"I was lucky that Master wanted me, I was nothing special, nothing out of the ordinary. May I sit down?" She was interested to know what people were saying about her.

The man moved slightly to allow her to perch on the end of the bench, he took a long drag on his cigar and allowed tiny rings of smoke escape from his lips. His new companion felt her legs open automatically until they were twelve inches apart at the knee, her hands rested in her lap and she bowed her head slightly. At the start of the evening she had made a mental note that she would be not be paraded like property fresh to the market, the demonstration with Anthony had managed to set most of the Dom's straight.

"You were not at the dinner, are you not a guest?" she wanted to know; the man simply took a draw on his cigar and smiled.

"I was invited but this isn't my scene, if I have a submissive why would I need the company of others except to show her off?" The words were familiar to China, this man could almost have been J in his mannerisms. Her curiosity started to get the better of her as they talked until eventually she couldn't contain herself any longer.

"Did you know my Master well? You seem so alike." She sat back relieved that she had asked, relaxing as she waited for the answer.

"Yes I knew him many years ago, before he cut himself off from the world."

"Did you know him very well?" she pushed, searching for an answer in his face.

"At one time I knew him very well, probably better than he knew himself." The sentence puzzled China and she sat motionless waiting for the man to expand on the answer. "At one time he was my best friend."

China woke with a start, the alarm clock flashed seven thirty and she struggled to her feet. As the memory of the previous evening swam into her head she wondered if she had dreamt it, there were no marks on her wrists or ankles and it was only when she looked in the mirror that she saw little red blotch's made by the wax starting to fade. Her body prickled with the thrill of recollection and she wished that she did not have to go to work.

In the kitchen she boiled the kettle and settled down to read the paper, she ate well and as she started to dress in her work clothes she noticed a small note pinned to the bathroom mirror, 'China, I shall meet you at Madam Sophia's premises at exactly 6 O'clock, she is expecting you. Master.' China felt her heart quicken, if she was returning to the shop then J was obviously buying her new outfits.

She pulled on her skirt and blouse, a rather dull bra lifted her heavy breasts and she hated the restraints of the vanilla world, she longed to stay with her Master, to roam around the flat as he wished. As she sat on the stool and applied her make-up she could not help but let her mind wander, she was aware of the hot flashes running through her body. China looked back at J as he slept, gradually she couldn't stop herself slipping the skirt up until she sat in her bare cheeks. Her fingers teased apart her lips and she sucked her fingers greedily before she slipped them between her legs, pressing her clitoris and grinding herself slowly and rhythmically against the flat of her hand. Panting uncontrollably she felt the rush of the orgasm and for a split second she was not sure if she would black out – it almost felt as if she was about to hit a brick wall, cold shivers crawled across the small of her back and she stifled a groan by biting her lip.

"Master J," she sobbed as the muscles of her cunt gripped her fingers and she climaxed. For five minutes she sat rocking back and forth, her mind was clouded, body on fire with passion and desire. She wanted to slip between the sheets, to guide his cock between her legs, to feel him deep inside her again. The material of the bra rubbed her nipples as she breathed and that only made it worse. She caught sight of the clock and pulled herself together, the rest of the day would be filled with daydreams but right now she needed to concentrate, she needed to make it out the door into the cold morning air and then she could settle into her everyday routine.

Forcing herself to fix her make-up China couldn't help but smile, she was alive inside, Gill was gone and replacing the timid, businesslike girl was China. Bold ,unafraid, ready to put her complete trust and safekeeping in the hands of another, she wasn't sure of the future but that didn't matter, all that did matter was a simple fact. She was where she belonged.

THIRTEEN

China turned off the main street and into the back road towards Madam Sophia's shop; she passed the girl begging and looked down at her. She remembered that J had spoken to her and felt a little jealous; reaching into her bag she took a couple of pound coins and squatted in front of the girl. She examined the beggar's wrists for a second before looking into the girl's eyes.

"What are these marks?" China asked tenderly running her fingers down the girl's arm to the raw skin around her wrists.

"Penance," came the simple answer. China thought for a second the girl meant that she was cutting herself but then discounted the notion.

"Penance for what?" China pushed; she dropped the coins into the girl's filthy hand and watched her eyes for signs of an answer.

"Penance for being vain, for being a whore, for not being a good girl, I didn't do as I was told." The words were a shock to China and she stood up quickly. If this girl had been discarded then it could happen to her, realisation flooded her thoughts and she took a long look across at the tiny door.

"Was Madam Sophia your mistress?" The girl shook her head.

"All gone, no-one is coming back for Sam," the despair in the beggar's voice filled China with dread and she fled to the safety of the shop.

She knocked quickly and squeezed inside when one of the servants opened the door. Without being told she stripped away the layers of her working outfit and stood naked, waiting for J to arrive. One of Madam Sophia's helpers strolled through the door and took her hand; she was led up a spiral staircase to a larger room. Madam Sophia waited patiently in one corner of the, she peered out the window before crossing to where China waited.

"What did the child on the street tell you?" The crop in Madam's hand flicked out and caught China's chin, she used the tip to raise the subs face. "She told me she had been abandoned after displeasing somebody, and that no-body wanted her."

Satisfied that China spoke the truth Madam Sophia closed the blinds and clicked her fingers, her servants instantly attended to her placing a wide collar and chain into her outstretched hand. She examined it for a moment and nodded her head. The elder of the two girls took the collar and wrapped it around China's neck tightening it until it fitted correctly. "Your Master will join us later, right now I have been asked to demonstrate the power of a Mistress."

China shook openly, Madam's crop was now running over her body, it flicked her nipples and rested between her legs. The servants held out China's arms as their Mistress examined every inch of the subs body before reaching a verdict.

"Put her on the 'A' frame, cheeks out."

The wooden frame dwarfed the submissives as they fastened China in place with her hands above her head. She prayed that they were not intending to whip her and turned her head slightly so that she could watch Madam Sophia in a mirror. The Domme picked up various paddles and crops until finally she was left with a fierce looking cane and a leather paddle.

"Your Master mentioned that your anus has not been trained, is that correct?" China nodded, she felt weak and vulnerable, aware that all three women were watching her, "I think we will start there,"

China felt her buttocks opened and cold, light lubricant was applied to her tight anus. She pulled away trying to avoid the probing but bound tightly it was impossible to escape and eventually she felt the tip of the small plug pushing inside her.

84

"Your Master may wish to take his pleasure from you in such a way, you must be ready." China was shocked to see in the mirror that the plug was attached to a small tail, Madam pulled it a little to ensure it was firmly in place and China clenched desperately, hoping it would not come free. As one of the servants placed a wide leather belt around her waist China saw for the first time a unique tattoo on the woman's shoulder, it looked so beautiful on her pale skin and China found herself openly staring at it. "You like that?" Madam asked, China nodded, "Beatrice... Show China your thigh."

The other servant came into sight and raised her tunic hem, an identical motif was displayed at the top of her thigh, "We wear it to honour our Mistress," she explained, "In the same way that you wear your Master's collar. This is the ultimate sign of our love and dedication."

Then Madam Sophia slowly unbuckled the intricately designed top she wore, her fingers sliding the garment from her shoulders to reveal the same design tattooed on her right breast, smaller, delicately coloured, but the same pattern all the same.

As China watched Madam raised the paddle and brought it down hard across her cheeks, the shock of the action forced her to suck in a lungful of air and she tried not to cry out, Beatrice held the China's chain in her hand, she tried hard not to meet China's eyes as the paddle pounded the tender white flesh of her buttocks. Each blow seemed to push the anal plug further inside her anus, she wondered if it would go all the way inside her, scared that she would be left with a tail.

The punishment continued until China lost count of the blows, her face was as hot as her buttocks; she had lost almost all feeling below the waist and had given up any thought of escape until finally Madam stopped.

"Release her," as the servants released China's arms they fell to her side and felt like lead; when they unbuckled her legs and waist she had little choice but fall to her knees exhausted.

Beatrice rubbed her arms legs until the blood circulated and feeling returned; China couldn't sit on her bruised buttocks so she knelt, her breasts swinging as she took panting breaths, aware that Beatrice still clung to her chain.

"Look at me," Madam Sophia ordered, China looked up to find her sitting on a wicker chair. One leg was draped over the arm and China blushed furiously at the sight of Madams cunt, she felt the first rush of excitement to her own sex and tried to maintain eye contact with the Domme. "Crawl to me now."

China did as she was told, each movement sending rushes of excitement through her body as the anal plug moved with the rhythm of her body, fucking her anus uncontrollably. She inched closer to Madam, her eyes gave away her desire to serve the powerful force in front of her and Sophia nodded at Beatrice – the chain fell to the floor as the woman went to carry out the Domme's subliminal wish.

"You want me," Madam stated, China's face went pink and she tried to look away.

"Yes Mistress." Sophia reached forward and took the loose chain hanging from China's collar, slowly, deliberately she winding it around her hand, pulling China ever closer.

"You may kiss my inner thigh and nothing else," eager China kissed and licked the woman's flesh, nibbling on the soft flesh as she tried to make Madam want her more, "Beatrice, you may fuck her."

China's head snapped up and looked at Sophia, the Domme stroked her own small firm nipples, pulling on the tiny rings that passed through them, she turned China's head with her fingertips until she caught sight of Beatrice in one of the many mirrors lining the room.

The servant had returned with a long dildo which her companion was strapping into place around her groin – it was so long that China wondered if it would damage her when it entered her cunt. Madam pulled the chain to draw the subs attention back to her, "You may lick me."

It wasn't an invitation more of an order and China found her head pulled further between the Domme's legs until her lips met the softness of Madams cunt, automatically she started to lick and suck, when she hurried Madam would slow her down, if she spent too long in one spot Madam would move her head. As she lapped eagerly at Sophia's sweet juice covered cunt she became aware that her lips were being parted, China held her breath for a minute and looked up.

"Please Mistress, let me please only you," she whispered, her hair was gripped as the Domme considered her request for a split second.

"No, I promised Beatrice that she could fuck you the first time you came to us, and I always keep my promises." Sophia pulled China's face back down and pushed up with her pelvis until it was very clear to the submissive that she was not going to have her way on this occasion.

As the dildo edged deeper and deeper China muffled her moans by concentrating on the cunt presented before her, she was aware that Sophia's grip had tightened and that her breathing was becoming laboured. She pushed her tongue deep inside and scooped out the Domme's juices; she had enjoyed the first time she had given pleasure to Teri, but this was different, a new heat and intensity raged through China's body and when she felt the first twinges of the climax it was too late to stop it. Her body buckled, she choked slightly and dug her nails into the ground as a cry burst from her lips. Trembling face down on the floor she felt the phallus slipping from her aching cunt, tears ran down her cheeks and she felt so ashamed that she had been unable to control her actions.

Cold air surrounded China as she lay on the floor, the room cooling, bathed in silence. The others had left to recover and now she felt the coldness of being alone, she hated it and stole a look around. In a plush leather chair J sat watching her, his fingers linked in his lap.

"Master? How long have you been there?" she asked as she staggered to her feet, the anal plug was gone and she hadn't felt it being removed.

"Long enough – you lasted longer than any other before your body gave up, I am very proud of you," he pulled her onto his lap and cradled her in his arms, her sore buttocks rested between his legs and cool air helped with the burning sensation.

"Madam Sophia is very demanding," China said, her arms were wrapped around his neck and their eyes met for a moment – China saw his feelings for her, the tenderness existed not in words but a look.

"She demands much, but she gives much in return."

China understood what he meant, Beatrice and the others had demonstrated that by taking her permanent mark and in an instant China made up her mind.

"Master, would you allow me to carry your mark?" She looked into his face for approval.

"You already carry my ownership." He answered, stroking her collar for a moment before returning her to his tender embrace.

"Master, I would like to carry a permanent symbol of your mark," she pushed, her nails dug into his flesh slightly.

For a long time they sat wrapped around each other, neither speaking, both enjoying the feeling until J broke the silence, "I will make the arrangements."

FOURTEEN

On their way home China told her Master about her meeting with the beggar girl – she wondered if J had any feelings about the girl's comments about penance. Curiosity plagued her mind, was Sam a rejected sub or was there a more sinister reason for her condition?

"You can't get her out of your head," J said out loud, it unnerved China that he seemed to be able to read her thoughts, she changed gear and pressed the accelerator in an effort to concentrate on other things.

"Would you like to know her story?"

"Did she tell you, Master?" China asked and she slowed the car down hoping that he would continue.

"No but I can tell you anyway. I would say that she is submissive and that those marks are the result of a badly trained Dom taking control of that naivety. I would say she gave herself completely and they used ropes and chains wrapped around her wrists and ankles to restrain her, I would also a hazard a guess to say that her back is marked by whip and cane. They drew blood."

China pulled the car over to the side of the road and turned to look at him. "Master that is a horrible scenario, why would you allow yourself to be subjected to such a thing?"

"You allowed your last Master to punish you almost so severely," J stated. China looked away for a moment, it was true but Anthony had stopped short of drawing blood.

The rest of their journey was conducted in silence, China remained lost in her memories of the past, fighting the feelings of revulsion that flooded her thoughts.

The next day when China finished work she drove around the streets trying to get the girl out of her mind and before she realised it she was parking outside Madam Sophia's shop looking across at the beggar's spot. The girl, filthy and shaking, sat in the rain with her blanket. Occasionally people would pass, even less frequently one or two would toss a few meagre coins to her.

China stepped from the car and pulled up an umbrella, upon leaving work she had put on her collar and now she made sure that it was visible above the collar of the coat she wore. She knelt down next to the girl; the beggar lifted her eyes and smiled before holding out her blanket for change. China took a moment to gather her feelings before speaking.

"I am going to offer you a home, it's warm and clean. In exchange I expect you to look after my Master." She spoke slowly and deliberately so there was no chance the girl could mishear, "You will make sure he is well looked after and in exchange you will be fed and cared for."

She pulled her coat down slightly so the girl had to acknowledge the collar's symbolism, "You understand why I wear this?"

"Yes, Ma'am," the voice was shaky and soft, big eyes looked up to meet China's, "Will I be punished?"

"Yes, if you require it. I cannot promise otherwise, but you will not be rejected."

The girl struggled to her feet, China held out her hand and helped her up, cold and wet the girl walked with a slight stoop towards the car. China opened the back door and ushered her inside; she took the girl's blanket and placed it in the boot, slipping off her coat and handing it to Sam.

"Get out of your wet clothes and put this on or you will catch your death of cold."

As they drove home China kept glancing in the mirror, the coat was far too big for Sam, she had pulled the sleeves down over her hands and buried her face in the collar – her tiny dirt covered face had streaks running down it where the rain and cleaned it. She kept looking out of the window noting where she was being driven. China reached into her bag and pulled out an untouched sandwich from lunch, she passed it back concentrating on the road. The rain was easing slightly, huge puddles of water erupted in spray as they drove through them, the noise making Sam jump every time.

"Nervous?" China asked, she turned up the heater.

"What do I have to do?" Sam asked, she took small nibbles at the bread and watched the back of China's head.

"You will cook, clean, ensure Master takes his medication and is all right whilst I am out." China explained, she turned the wheel into the drive and stopped.

"Do I have to fuck him?" Sam pressed her face to the glass and looked up at the flats.

"No.", China stepped out of the car and held open the door to allow Sam to clamber out. "Follow me."

Clutching her soaking coat to her chest Sam followed as China led her inside and up the stairs, when she unlocked the door Sam shuffled inside first before China followed and locked the door.

The beggar watched as China slipped out of her clothes and stood naked in the hall, she placed her clothes on the chair and led Sam into the kitchen.

"You are hungry?" she asked, the girl nodded and pulled her clothes tighter to her chest, "I suggest you empty the pockets and put them in the washing machine, if you decide not to stay then the least I can do is make sure you are clean and dry for a change."

When the girl had thought about it she emptied her pockets onto the table. China opened a carton of soup and poured the contents in a dish, as the microwave heated it she took Sam's clothes and pushed them as one ball into the washing machine.

"You need to take a bath, no point in you having clean clothes and a dirty body." China said as she took Sam's hand and led her into the bathroom, "You can lock the door if you wish and when you have finished you may put on the robe in the cupboard and come into the kitchen to eat."

When China left Sam slowly closed the door behind her and turned the key in the lock, she took a towel from the rail and placed it on the back of the bath and climbed in, hot water soaked into her skin and she drew a heavy breath, for the first time in months she felt warm. Taking a cake of soap she experimentally rubbed it down her arm and smelt it, there was no scent and that confused her a little. She cleaned herself thoroughly; leaning back in the back to wash her hair, as she lay in the water enjoying the sensation of being clean she was startled by a knocking on the door.

"Your soup will get cold if you don't hurry and the Master will be home shortly." China called.

Sam sat eating in silence, carefully watching China clean the kitchen – every sudden movement made her jump but eventually she settled. As the clock touched seven there came the sound of a key turning in the lock and China smiled, she placed her hand on Sam's shoulder and told her to stay seated as she went to greet the Master. Wide eyed the newcomer watched the door and waited as the lowered voices in the hallway came closer, and eventually J came into sight.

"Master, you remember Sam from the street outside Madam Sophia's?" China asked positioning herself behind the girl and resting both hands on the girls shoulders, "She has agreed to come and look after you."

J's eyes flared up in rage, "I do need a little girl to watch over me, I can take care of myself, we cannot stop time and her being here will simply cause clutter."

The tone of his words caused Sam to squeak in fright and she tried to stand, "Ok, Ma'am, thank you for the food and the bath but I think I will leave now."

As she stood the robe she wore slipped down with the weight of China's hands, scars long healed ran down and across her back, they were faded but still clearly visible.

"Sit down, Sam. I need to speak to the Master alone before I drive you back." China softly told the frightened girl before leading J into his study. The door closed as J almost fell into his chair, his face was pale and his hand gripped the arm of the chair.

"Master please, I want her," it was a bold statement that caused J to look long and hard at his submissive, he denied her nothing but pride still burned inside his soul. He knew if he allowed Sam to stay then she would tell China everything, but she would also be an asset in teaching his submissive further.

"Go and get her and take off that ridiculous robe," he spat, China nodded, bowed her head and did as he instructed, returning with Sam naked and trembling.

"You will only enter the kitchen, bathroom, bedroom and lounge. You will take instructions from China, you are her responsibility and should you fail in your duties she will be the one to carry out your punishment. Do you agree?"

Sam thought for a moment before nodding slowly, her hands rested across her pubic mound and she did not raise her gaze to meet J's.

"You will call me Master, or Sir, and I do not expect you to serve me outside of your courtesy, you are China's pet and will serve only her."

He turned and switched on the computer; sensing the meeting was over China took Sam and pulled her from the room.

"I will have to sort you out somewhere to sleep, and clothes for when you leave the house. Is there anything else you need?" China asked as they walked, Sam peeked into the rooms they passed trying to get her bearings in the place.

"Do I have to fuck him?" the statement was a simple one but it stopped China in her tracks.

"No, you do not touch the Master, not unless he requests you to," China said slowly, her eyes narrowed and filled with silent threat.

"What's wrong with him?" Sam asked, she didn't seem to see the look on China's face.

"I don't know exactly but you need to make sure he takes his medication and if he gets sick call the doctor, the number is by the phone. Under no circumstances call 999 without the doctor giving permission." Sam nodded and then continued into the kitchen.

China sat on the floor, her head resting in J's lap as his fingers stroked her hair tenderly.

"Master, where will she sleep?"

J thought for a moment, bending to kiss her forehead before answering, "She can sleep in the kitchen until you have trained her and then we can decide."

"I can't train her, Master; you must do it for me. Please." China reached out and scratched his beard, she wanted so much to make love to him, to feel him inside her and show her he wanted her.

"If I train her then she will not be yours, but I will be there to show you what to do and to ensure you do it correctly, under my control." He leaned back and a flicker of pain raced across his face.

"Master, she needs a lot of training, more than I did."

J's hand slithered down her chest and gently rolled her nipple, he stroked around it and teased it hard before his hand continued its journey down the flat of her stomach.

"You know you do not need that much training, you have done very well."

"But she does, you see it. Tell me what I have to do." China's voice was almost pleading.

"You will seduce her; make her want to serve you. She is already submissive, but she needs somebody to straighten out the mess she has already gone through. She needs you to be the anchor I was to you," J explained.

"Are to me, you are just what I need, want," she ran her fingers down his cheek and dug in her nails, J gripped her wrist and pulled her hand away, kissing her wrist.

Next morning China woke and walked into the kitchen – she expected to find Sam asleep on the bed she had made earlier but instead the girl was curled up in a corner in space barely big enough for a dog.

Gently China stroked the girls face until she woke, "Come, your duties start today and it's time to wake up." Sam nodded sleepily and unwrapped herself from the blanket, her pert breasts were red from the roughness of the material – she had ignored the duvet that J had given her.

"First things first, you must shower and shave, Master only permits us to be clean shaven or trimmed. You will be clean shaven to begin with." Sam nodded her head as they wandered into the bathroom, "Your hair must be pulled back from your face, I will take you to have it cut soon but in the meantime you have such a pretty face it would be a shame to hide it."

China turned on the shower and handed Sam a razor, pushing the girl into the cubicle she climbed in next to her. Laughing Sam turned her back on the older woman and pretended to hide herself, China started to massage her companions shoulders and back, working the soap into a thick lather, her fingers worked down the girls back and between her legs until her index finger gently pushed against Sam's anus causing her to squeal slightly.

"Please, I have been thinking about you all night. May I kiss you?" Sam begged as she turned her head slightly, placing her hands on the glass.

Her lips parted and she panted heavily, unconsciously she ran the tip of her tongue around her lips and turned her head as far as she could, "Please kiss me."

China placed her hands on either side of the girl, her breasts rubbed against Sam's back and slid her hands down to follow the outline of the girl's body. The palms of her hands stroked the former beggar's small breasts, she ran her long nails around the girl's nipples and then down her stomach, resting just above Sam's pelvis.

Sharply China pulled Sam back, grinding her pelvis against Sam's back, pseudo fucking the girl under the hot jets of water. As the newcomers head fell back between China's breasts she moaned slightly.

"Do you want me?" China whispered in her ear, Sam shook and nodded her head, she stood on tiptoes in an effort to move China's hands further south down her body.

"Good, the you will do as you are told and obey me, now shave you have to help me prepare for work." Sam let out a cry of frustration as China stepped out of the shower and left her alone to wash and shave.

Sitting on the stool China watched and waited for Sam to finish; when she stepped from the shower China re-entered the cubicle and closed the door.

"Dry yourself and lay out my make-up on the top, quietly go and get my suit from the bedroom, it's hanging up behind the door – don't wake Master up." China called over the top of the cubical; through the glass she watched Sam scuttle away to carry out her tasks and smiled, she was happy, very happy.

Sam had returned by the time China emerged – she crossed the room and stood in front of her pet and held out the towel to Sam.

"Dry me." Sam did as she was told, her fingers expertly moved the towel across China's skin, it lingered for a second between her legs before

Sam snatched her hand away when she realised and stepped back in embarrassment.

"Sorry… I didn't mean…" she stammered trying not to look China in the face.

Sitting down with her back to the girl China took the eye-shadow, lipstick and highlighter pencil and demonstrated to Sam how each needed to be applied; then she handed the girl a hairbrush and sat straight backed as the bristles stroked their way through her hair.

"Tomorrow you will apply my make-up, brush my hair and get my clothes ready without prompting, you will learn the correct routine quickly and then we will move on in your training." China watched the girl's face in the mirror, she stared longingly as the brush pulled through China's dark locks, she stood closer than she needed and China felt the girl's hard nipples pressing into her back.

When she had finished she stepped back, China turned her head to make sure it looked as good as when she did it, then swivelled round on the stool.

"Stockings first, then bra, skirt and finally blouse. I always wear black heels for work, boots if Master wishes me to go somewhere after work."

Wide eyed Sam watched as China took a pen from the side and carefully applied J's mark to the top of her thigh, when she finished it was a little lopsided so she took a wipe and rubbed it off.

"Come here, Sam." Quickly the young sub came around and knelt between China's legs, she was then handed the pen, "The Master's mark is an 'X' with a 'J' running through it, carefully write it here." China pressed the tip of her nail against her soft thigh and watched as Sam very carefully did as she was told.

"Am I allowed to wear his mark?" she asked innocently, China cupped the girl's chin in her hand and looked into her eyes.

"That is something you must ask him, but I think you can expect the answer to be 'no.'" China brushed her lips against Sam's, teasing her with a kiss that never happened, "You may dress me now."

Letting out a shallow groan of frustration Sam rose and retrieved each article of clothing in order of priority. As her nimble fingers smoothed the stockings up China's thighs, she paused to place a single kiss at the top of each ring of support elastic. Gently she cupped China's breasts from behind and lifted them into the bra, pausing for a second to clip the clasp together. She found it strange seeing China dressed in this way, somehow it didn't seem natural. Once the bra was in place China stood, legs apart and stepped into the skirt, before she allowed Sam to draw it up she took her pets chin in her fingers and drew the girl between her legs, with a shallow whimper Sam started to lick gently, her tongue exploring the sweet recesses of China's sex until it located the clitoris.

"Would you like to taste me?" China asked, she had drawn Sam's head back and the strain was showing on the sub's face.

"Please, Mistress, please let me have you," she begged, her nails dug into China's leg but it made no difference.

"I am no Mistress, not even yours. Say my name." China told her.

"China," at the sound of the words China pulled her flushed face between her legs and allowed her to taste the sweet juices that flowed freely from China's cunt. Within seconds China climaxed, through her gritted teeth she called out, "Master J."

Gripping Sam's head so that she couldn't move China held her close until the orgasm subsided and her body stopped trembling.

"Fetch my blouse, I'm going to be late," she released Sam from her grip and struggled to pull up the skirt, as the blouse was slipped over her arms, "Look after Master, do as he tells you."

She kissed Sam on the lips, allowing herself to taste her own juices before slipping into her shoes and running for the door.

Going to work was easy, her employers had been good enough to allow her to transfer to an office close by but it was an autonomous existence, dull and mind numbing. The people she dealt with nine-to-five were relatively uninteresting but she found herself seeing them as either dominants or submissives, and was glad when she made the transition back to China.

Left alone in the house Sam went back to her bed. Curled in the corner she tucked her hand between her legs and started to tease her cunt apart. Her index finger gently stroked along her lips, they felt hot and sticky causing Sam to smile. Using two fingers she drew back the hood of her clit, it was tender and wet, slowly she pressed the exposed little pink button. Her heart raced and her breathing became heavy as she massaged it, her nipples were already swollen and hard, using her free hand she gripped her leg and cried out as the climax hit, her stomach was knotted with nerves and her buttocks clenched as the force of her orgasm refused to subside. Involuntarily her pelvis pushed up, forcibly fucking her fingers until the next one arrived. As it ripped through her small body Sam pulled her fingers away and slipped them into her mouth to enjoy the sweet nectar that covered them.

A slow clap rang out around the kitchen; when she dared open her eyes J stood watching her.

"Obviously, China did not explain the rule about not climaxing without permission," shame faced Sam shook her head. "Ignorance is no excuse, you will take punishment… or you can leave if you wish."

The bottom of Sam's stomach felt like stone, she had only been there less than twenty-four hours and it already appeared that J did not approve of her presence; a fire swelled in her heart. China wanted her, she was sure of that and there was no way she was going to allow J to stand in the way.

"Punishment," she said abruptly, defiant in her tone.

"Punishment… what?"

"Punishment, SIR," she glowered at him across the room as she answered.

FIFTEEN

China smiled as she climbed the stairs, she was looking forward to relaxing for the evening – as far she knew her Master had nothing organised and it would be nice just to sit and listen to music, curled up in his lap with a book.

The first thing she noticed when she walked in was the quietness, not a sound broke the still air. In the kitchen Sam's bed had been tidied away and she became worried that the girl had left without saying goodbye. When she turned she noticed that Sam's clothes were still neatly piled on the chair and her curiosity turned to anger as she pushed open the bedroom door.

Her expectation at finding the missing pair in bed was dashed; the bed lay empty and cold. She pressed on eager to find her Master, finally she turned the handle to the playroom, it's interior remained bathed in half-light and kneeling in the centre of the room, bound to a stool by her thighs and wrists was Sam.

"Master?" J stepped from behind the door and pushed it closed. His arm wrapped around China's waist and he kissed her passionately. Pressing back she could feel the hardness of his cock pressing her cheeks through his trousers.

"She needs to be punished, I caught her touching herself." China rounded on him, the palm of her hand rested on his cheek and she searched his eyes.

"She didn't know, Master. I have yet to explain the rules to her. This isn't really fair." He took her hand in his and kissed it slowly, moving away from her.

She watched him take up a paddle and in disbelief he handed it to her.

"I told you that you would be responsible for her training, six strokes."

Slowly China took the handle and felt the weight, the surface of the paddle was broad and thin, it weighed very little and she guessed that it was designed for shock more than pain, she nodded and went to Sam, kneeling in front of her face.

"You understand you are to be punished, do you agree?" She looked deep into Sam's face and hoped she understood.

"Yes, China. I accept my punishment," she stated.

China took up her position behind the bound sub and raised the paddle; it came down swiftly and cleanly, catching the flesh square on. Sam squeaked in shock, raising her head to call out then thought better of it. Each smack raised the temperature of her cheeks and made them go redder and redder but as quickly as she started China stopped. Carefully she bent forward and kissed the girls burning cheeks before standing up and handing back the paddle to J.

"Do you require anything else, Master?" she asked, J placed the paddle on the table.

"You think I have been unfair?"

"No, Master. You know what is best for us," China replied, she couldn't look at him, her attention was focused on the wall on the other side of the room. J lifted her face and drew himself close to her ear, "You may climax." China fought the spasms running through her thighs but she knew she couldn't hope to control it, her cry of pleasure filled the room and Sam tried desperately to look round to see what was happening, without success.

Gripping J's arm to stay upright China kissed his shoulder, "Master J." she cried softly.

Paul tossed his cigar into the ashtray by the door and turned his attention back to China. For the first time he took a long hard look at her. She was not what he expected, he had heard the gossip and the rumours, but China was far from the timid little sub he had been lead to believe she was.

Anthony had taken great delight in being salacious in his boasting of how he had tamed her, something that Paul found very hard to believe.

"Tell me about my Master when he was younger, was he always so gifted?" her question brought wild laughter from Paul.

"J always had a way about him, even in our teens he would be a little dark and mysterious; eager to share only the smallest details of his conquests." China looked crestfallen; she had heard that J enjoyed the company of women to a high degree and now jealousy burned in the pit of her stomach.

"So he had fucked a lot of women?" China asked, her face had gone stone hard and she refused to look at Paul directly, he simply drew another cigar and slipped it between his lips.

"God no, for your Master the thrill was in the hunt, the topping. A simple fuck was not part of the equation, it was all about control," Paul explained, his match flared in the fast approaching darkness and a plume of grey enveloped them and stopped the midges from biting, "You orgasmed when he told you to."

"How did you know?" She sounded surprised at his question, it was not something she told friends never mind strangers.

"I know a lot about many things, and I have seen J produce quite spectacular results."

China shifted uneasily in her seat, Paul had fixed his gaze on her and refused to break it, it was disturbing how he seemed to probe her soul for answers, "May I see the mark?"

China stood and lifted exposed her cheeks, Paul's fingers followed every line and curve; finally he spoke.

"And if you find another Master, what is he to think?"

"I hope he feels that this is a demonstration of my commitment to my role, and ultimately him. Most of all I hope is proud to own a sub trained by one of the finest Master's."

Sam woke and opened her eyes, she had spent the night sleeping on her front but had turned over in her sleep and she became aware of the heat flooding down to her buttocks.

Looking at the clock above the stove she suddenly panicked, J had given her special instructions on how to serve China in the morning and she was in danger of failing. She stepped out of bed, tidied it away and splashed water over her face to freshen up.

As quietly as she could she made her way into the bedroom, J slept with his arm across China as she lay on her side. Slowly Sam crept onto the bed – J stirred and half woke, he looked down the bed and rolled away from China, his arm drawing her onto her back. Even in sleep China slept with her legs apart when able and Sam slipped between her legs easily.

Following J's instructions Sam crept higher and higher, when she reached the top of China's thighs she slid her hands under the sleeping subs legs and inched forward. The tip of her tongue flicked out, it nudged its way along China's labia, pushing deep inside her gently. The sleeper let out a moan of desire and opened her legs further allowing Sam to move into position, she closed her lips around China's cunt and sucked.

The sleeper's breathing quickened, her hands moved to her stomach and she stroked herself, deep inside the realisation dawned of what was happening to her and China opened her eyes and looked down expecting to see J kneeling between her legs. The sight that greeted her caught her by surprise and she leaned back, pushing her pelvis up to meet Sam's actions. "Oh, yes." She cried quietly, J opened his eyes fully and watched the scene for a moment before slipping from the bed. His arm disappeared between Sam's legs from behind and two fingers opened her cunt. Expertly he circled her clitoris with his index finger, she was already wet and matched his fucking with her own movement against China; she chanced a breath. "Please may I cum?" she hissed urgently, "please China, may I?"

China was fighting for her own breath, her heart was pounding and in her direct line of sight she could see the effect that J was having on Sam. "Master, may I climax?" China asked, she knew that should Sam orgasm first it would set her off.

"Yes you may." He never took his eyes off her, watching every expression that passed across her face.

"Now, Sam," as the words left her throat Sam let out a long, deep moan and clamped her mouth firmly to China's groin.

As China predicted her own climax was intense and unstoppable, she gripped Sam's hair and played with her nipples, squeezing them in turn. J's hard cock look so inviting that China suddenly realised she was desperate to taste it, to feel it deep inside her in one way or another.

"Please make love to me, Master," China begged, her hand reaching out towards him but J simply took it and kissed it.

"Tonight, sweet China, tonight."

"Please, My Master, take me now." She pulled away from Sam and hauled herself up onto her elbows hooking her legs onto the end of the bed and offering herself to him.

Silently J stood, he did not turn his back on her, he simply backed from the room and kept eye contact until he reached the door, his finger closed around the handle and the door swung shut.

J worked long through the day, he wrote tirelessly in the morning before pain overtook him and he was forced to stop. He took lunch in his study and fell into an uneasy sleep. Outside the heat of the day meant many of the passerby's wore thin summer clothes but J shivered and felt the slightest cold. As the clock on the wall struck three he woke and changed, ordered Sam to fetch him a thin cotton shirt and his waistcoat. From the cupboard he fished out the battered leather jacket.

"I shall be back at eight, bath and dry China, do not allow her to climax at any time. She will be hypersensitive but I want her to wait. Do you understand?" Sam nodded but did not look him in the eye, she felt something was wrong, "Tell her I wish her to present herself for me, she will know what it means."

"Excuse me, Sir. What would you like me to do tonight?" Sam asked. J turned to look her in the eye.

"You will serve."

He turned and left and for long minutes Sam stood waiting for something – it seemed wrong that she had to wait for so long before China came home, she felt at ease taking instructions – she needed them.

China sat in the bath and relaxed. When she had come home Sam had told her exactly the instructions J had given her, word for word. A smile had stretched across her lips and Sam looked puzzled.

"Master taught me how to present myself when I first met him, before I… well before we parted for the first time," China explained.

The younger sub perched on the end of the bath, her hand trailed up China's thigh until it reach the top, she wanted to go further but J had warned against it.

"You have such a pretty name, who chose it your Mother or your Father?" Sam asked, her index finger gently running down China's lips towards her anus and automatically China clenched.

"China is the name Master gave me, he said it suited me," she laughed, her hand shot out and placed a smudge of foam on Sam's nose. "Now stop tormenting me with those fingers and go and get me a towel."

Sam did as instructed, returning with the towel clutched close to her naked chest, "China, what did he mean when he mentioned 'presenting'?"

"He is bringing a guest or guests home tonight and I need to put on my make-up and be ready to serve, if I look good then it makes Master proud."

"What do you wear?"

"You will see," China patted herself dry and went to the make-up table, she sat down and handed Sam the brush.

Carefully she followed the same routine she did in the morning, slowly, methodically applying her lipstick and eye shadow. Sam watched in the mirror, there was no doubt in her mind that China was very beautiful, why she chose to serve J was a little hard to understand, after all Sam was sure that China could have her pick of men.

"How do you feel when, Sir allows others to see you?" her head was to one side and she had slowed down her brush strokes.

"I am proud to serve him; he makes me feel complete, makes me feel special and wanted."

Sam's eyes drifted down, hypnotically she watched China circle her areola with the highlighter pencil, then filled it in with the lipstick. Once she had finished she took the stick and the thinnest line was applied to her labia. Shocked and open-mouthed, Sam could only watch as China stood and turned to show herself. Her eyes looked darker, thin lines traced back and China's features had taken on almost an Egyptian appearance. Slowly she placed her leg on the stool and pulled on a brand new pair of self-supporting stockings before finally placing a silver collar around her neck.

"What do you think?" she asked, Sam couldn't find the words to describe the desire she felt, a few simple lines had changed China from a beautiful woman into a stunning woman.

"And people will see you like this tonight?" Sam asked in disbelief.

"Yes, they will see me, desire me, and know that I belong to Master J in every way." Finally she took the marker from the top and handed it to Sam, "Put J's mark on my thigh, you know I shake too much."

As Sam's hand drew the 'X' and ran the 'J' through it she stole a single kiss at the top of China's thigh.

They both heard the car doors close and quickly left the bathroom; Sam remained completely naked and blushing she kept her hands in front of her and trying to keep as much of herself covered as was possible.

"Don't worry, they will see you but they will not show it. Now put your hands in the small of your back, legs apart and look relaxed," China whispered just as the door opened.

J was the first to enter, when he saw China he smiled slightly and nodded his approval, she knew instinctively that he was delighted with her appearance and she had not failed; behind him a scruffy looking man followed. In his hand he gripped a black case but when China tried to take it along with his coat he refused. Curiosity swelled inside her but it didn't show. The man looked her over and called out to her Master.

"I see your reputation for beautiful Slaves is not exaggerated, she is a fine looking sub."

J turned to look at her for a second before answering, "Yes, she is the finest. Sam, take our guest into the playroom."

The young sub led the way leaving her peers standing in the corridor; once the door had closed behind her China spoke.

"Master, may I ask a question?" J poured himself a drink and thought for a moment.

108

"You may."

"He is not the usual guest I would expect, he seems less, well, refined, out of place."

J placed the glass on a coaster and walked towards the playroom door, "Yes, tonight I am going to give you a gift to show how much you mean to me."

The playroom walls seemed darker – J had placed China in the middle of the room and ordered Sam to lock her thighs into the heavy frame - confused and numb China allowed herself to be manipulated. The thick leather strap that stretched around her waist felt cold to the skin and she remembered how she had felt when J had first put her in it, the hot wax, the sensation of raw passion mixed with total control.

Once her wrists and ankles were fastened in China expected them to be turned horizontal but instead J removed his jacket. She watched in horror as their guest opened his case and laid out a tattooing needle and ink; he slipped on a pair of rubber gloves and walked towards China, inches from her face he stopped.

"Your favourite colour?" he asked, she pulled back and tried not to look at him, his breath smelt of stale cigarettes and beer. Rough stubble was trying its best to make his face look like sandpaper. China cringed.

"Dark purple or mottle green" she answered – he brought the needle gun up in front of her eyes.

"You can scream, I've heard it all before," he warned.

He turned and walked back towards J, needle gun raised slightly, he picked up a small bottle of ink and screwed it in place.

"You picked right. You do know your Slave, let's see if she expected this," as the man spoke J turned his back on them, his fingers fought the buttons on his shirt and eventually it fell to the floor.

He sat on a stool and bent forward, in horror China watched as the tattooist started his work, the needles piercing J's shoulder and injecting the layers of ink. China strained at the straps holding her, she wanted to see what was going on, she wanted to hold J in her arms, feeling his pain as he took it without a sound. The man was right she did want to scream, this was worse than her own punishments.

Eventually she gave up and relaxed, watching the quick and careful way the man worked, his movements seemed so sure, and he worked quickly until after half an hour he had finished.

"There, it will need a couple of days to heal but it will be fine if you keep it covered and keep it clean," he stated. As he stepped out of China's line of sight she let out a cry of astonishment.

On J's shoulder an intricate 'C' gave way to smaller letters that spelt out her name, tears welled up in her eyes and she heard Sam gasp at the sight.

"Release her, Sam, and then show our guest out." J instructed as he stood up. He closed his eyes for a second and the tattooist reached out to support him.

"You all right, man?" he asked. J focused on his face for a moment and then placed his hand on his shoulder.

"Yes, I think I am for the first time in a very, very long time. Thank you. I think I just stood up a bit quickly."

Once free China dashed to her Master's side, her fingers explored his shoulder, running around the broken skin, her eyes flicked across his face looking for signs of pain but found none.

"Why, Master?" she whispered as the tattooist was being escorted out by Sam. China placed tiny kisses around his mouth.

"Because I wanted to show you how much you mean to me, my sweet little girl." His fingers followed the outline of her eyes and down her nose; he placed his lips to hers and kissed her warmly and passionately. The intensity of the action made her feel hot and flushed, her toes scrunched up on the hard floor as she pushed up to meet him. She pulled back, her eyes were closed and she held her heart in her mouth; the red coating of her nipples had rubbed against J's chest and she bent slightly to kiss the marks, the tip of her tongue darted out touched his skin. This was the first time she had been allowed to freely explore his body, to touch him without him telling her what to do.

J took her hand and led her into the bedroom, as Sam appeared he closed the door in her face.

SIXTEEN

China stood at the end of the bed with her back to her Master, J stroked her curves, his hands touched every part of her skin so gently it was almost like the caress of a butterfly and she shivered from head to toe. Every pore of her body cried out to be touched, a single kiss was placed in the small of her back and automatically her labia swelled and prickled with desire, one bead of sweat rolled down her forehead and down the side of her nose, without thinking her tongue flicked out and followed the outline of her lips.

J moved his hands further down the tops of China's thighs, his fingers moved between her legs and parted them further. Without a single instruction China bent forward, she pushed her buttocks towards him and moaned softly as his tongue followed the curves of her cheeks. In a haze of desire China put her hands flat on the bed, opened her legs further and offered the soft folds of her cunt to him, for long moments he made her wait and then he caressed them with the tip of his tongue. China's cry started in her chest and surged upwards, her breathing quickened to the point where she thought her lungs would burst and her arms buckled.

As she lay panting face down on the bed J continued with his task, his tongue flicking backwards until it pressed her anus, she pulled in as much air as she could, the shakes started in her legs and burst upwards, as J pushed his tongue into her buttocks she cried out with pleasure and climaxed, wave upon wave passed through her body.

Gently China found herself being turned onto her back, trembling and weak she tried to help but found herself easily moved. The world seemed to fade around them, she saw J looking down on her and watched in slow motion as he removed his trousers. She reached out and placed his hard cock in the palm of her hand, slowly she ran her hand down to his balls. They felt heavy and soft; pulling gently she moved him up the bed and guided the tip towards her soft mouth. It was all she could do to lift her head, her lips took him willingly and she gorged herself, her mouth suckling gently on the tip before sinking her mouth as far down as she could.

China appealed for more with her eyes, she knew that talking was beyond her ability at the moment and hoped J understood the desire in her face. Smiling he moved back down the bed, his hands dug under her back and seconds later he lifted her high enough from the bed to help her shuffle up to the pillows. Before she could be enveloped in the depths of the bedclothes J pulled a pillow from under her head and slipped it under her buttocks, raising her lower body up slightly.

"Master?" Her mouth barely moved; her voice little more than a whisper, "Please…"

Her words were lost as J slipped between her legs; he kissed her mouth, biting her sensitive lips. China's hands stretched out on his back, she was conscious of the new tattoo and tried her best to avoid it. As J moved down he kissed and bit her skin, sucking on her sweat coated flesh. Every hair on her body stood on end; her blood seemed to boil as J suckled greedily on her hard nipples. Uncontrollably China's body ground itself against J's body and the Dom took full advantage of his charge's state and pulled back slightly, the tip of his cock resting against her lower stomach. China was already stretching back in an effort to move him downwards – when the desired effect refused to work she opened her eyes – J looked down on her, the corners of his mouth curled in a slight smile.

"Tell me what you want?"

"Please, Master," she groaned pushing up her pelvis, "Please, Master. Fill me."

Her hand skimmed her stomach as she moved her hand down; it reached the tip of his cock and placed it between her lips. "Make love to me, Master. Show me you want me…"

Inch by inch J started to ease himself inside her; his head dropped between her breasts and he kissed her cleavage, his teeth biting her tender skin. Once he was fully inside J placed his arms under her knees and lifted her legs allowing his gorging cock to push deeper, filling her completely. As they moved together China gripped his hair to hold him still – she wanted to hold him just for a moment, to enjoy the feeling of being complete.

"I love you so much, Master," she breathed before relaxing her hold allowing J to continue, his body subtly moved against hers, every fresh contact causing her body to respond. China closed her eyes so tight that tiny sparks of light danced under the lids. She felt J relax for a moment and became worried that he was about to climax, forcing her eyes to open in time to watch him pull out.

"Master, is something wrong?" she asked huskily, J reached up and kissed her tender lips, China tasted her own juice on his lips before he pulled back and smiled.

"No, nothing is wrong. Turn over, China," the sound of her name sent waves of pleasure tumbling down her spine and she did as she was told. The pillow that had lifted her from the bed now raised her buttocks and China was left wondering if J was about to take her anally.

Gently he closed her legs, the gesture confused her and China turned her head slightly to watch him in the mirror. Carefully J lowered himself on top of her, one arm rested on the bed by her head whilst the other eased his throbbing cock between her legs. For a few precious seconds she was sure that he would try and enter her anus and she bit her lip in readiness of the stretching pain but it didn't happen. Instead she became aware that the tip of his cock was slipping along her vaginal opening. J's thighs were gripping her legs shut, holding her tight, she breathed out just as he eased this long shaft deep inside her.

This sensation was new to China and she cried out in pleasure. Once J was fully inside her he lowered his body down to cover hers, both hands now rested on either side of her head and he started to pump slowly. His cock seemed to grow inside her, the edge of the pillow was rubbing her tender clit and breathing was becoming difficult. Every time China felt him as deep as he could be, in the millisecond before he pulled away, she thought she was going to explode. Intense heat filled her body, the muscles in her cunt throbbed and burned, desperately holding onto her Master before allowing him to pull away and continue.

Finally it became too much and China heard herself begging to climax, sweat covered her mouth and as she spoke she tasted it on her lips. Her words seemed so quiet that she was unsure that her Master would hear them, but J had and he kissed the back of her neck, his face came close to her ear and he whispered so softly that is was almost a thought in her head.

"You may climax, China."

Her fingers gripped the covers and she buried her face in the pillows, biting as her entire body rocked from the released explosion of energy. Tears streamed down her face and her body gripped him refusing to release.

J lifted himself slightly from her body permitting her to breathe freely but she could only suck in air as small pants. The force of her next climax seemed small but no less intense – this time she felt her muscles contract allowing J to push in fully again and he held himself there as the climax hit. China woke on her side, she tried hard to remember what had happened next but everything was a fog. Placing her hand behind her back she felt J – as always he lay close, almost in the curves of her body. His presence comforted her and she pressed back with her buttocks. His cock still felt hard against her cheeks and she let out a sigh of desire.

J's hand rested across her stomach and China slipped from his embrace and left the room. The darkness surround her as she made her way to the bathroom and she looked through the kitchen door to check on Sam. The girl was missing; frantically China walked from room to room, there was just enough light from the moon coming through the window to allow her to see shapes, but she couldn't find Sam anywhere. She felt a mixture of emotions, on one hand she was upset that her pet had left, on the other had she would be alone with her Master and that meant no distractions.

She sat on the toilet and looked around, the mirrors glistened, plants on the window ledge cast dangerous shadow creatures onto the far wall and she watched them dance in a the breeze caused by the gap in the open window. A floorboard creaked and she looked up to see J standing in the door, he smiled at her, it was one of the few times she had seen him looking happy. He lifted his hand and placed his finger to his lips motioning her to remain silent. Then he beckoned her to follow him.

Silently China followed, picking her steps carefully so that the floor didn't give her away; when she reached the passage she could see J waiting for her by the bedroom door. He had pushed it open slightly and through the crack she could see Sam asleep on the floor at the foot of the bed, her hands snuggled into the crook of her elbow, cover pulled up close to her chin. China wasn't sure how she had missed her when she left the room but the young sub looked so peaceful and content where she lay that China was almost glad that she hadn't stepped on her. J closed the door quietly and padded into the kitchen, for a big man he moved quite gracefully, he pulled out a chair for China and she sat down, her hands resting in her lap. She watched him making coffee and noted that he was very much at ease naked. Once when J had slept and she had woken early she had passed her time running her nails down any of the many scars she could find. Now as he prepared their drinks she tried to remember them all, one or two were easy, big enough to see in plain sight whilst others remained hidden under hair or in little crevices on his body.

"What are you thinking?" he asked as he placed her cup down on the table, his hand running down her chin to lift it so he could look into her eyes.

"I was thinking about many things, J." She placed her head on one side to look at him. He sat at the head of the table looking at her, sometimes he looked stern, but now he looked like a concerned parent.

"What will you do when I am gone?" he whispered, China took his hand and kissed his wrist. For a long time they seemed to ignore the issue of his health but both knew it couldn't be put off for much longer.

"You will never leave me, Master," she replied coyly. Instinctively she reached out to hold his hand, prising it from the hot cup of coffee.

"Won't I?"

"No, you will always be with me." She kissed his large fingers, biting them gently. "Promise me you will." She rested her head on his hand and watched his face.

"My dearest China, I will watch over you forever. You will never be alone." She smiled and stood up, pulled his legs out from under the table and sat down on his lap. She placed her arms around his neck and kissed him passionately, her breasts pressed tight against his chest and he wrapped his arms around her waist. They sat until daybreak in a warm embrace, disturbed only by the sound of the birds.

"We have an invite to a party, do you want to go?" The words stirred China from her thoughts and she looked across the table as J read out the post.

"What?"

"We have been invited to a gallery opening; your friend Mary has sent us an invite. Shall we go?" he asked again. The memory of Mary's betrayal burned in her mind for a minute as she thought it over. She remembered it was the first time she had laid eyes on J, how taken she was with him that first time, how much she wanted him.

"I shall leave it to your judgement, Master," she stood and walked behind him, the tattoo of her name was fast healing and wondered if other Dom's thought so highly of their charges that they etched their names for eternity on their bodies, she guessed not.

"I shall have Sam pick up something from Madam Sophia's, a surprise," he picked up his toast and bite down hard. China watched him earnestly, she had been trying to make him eat as per the doctor's orders and he had always fought her. Since they had made love for the first time she noticed he was following the correct diet. Colour had returned to his cheeks and his moods had picked up, his permanent depression seemed to have passed.

"Master can I not go to Madam Sophia's, do you not trust my choice in attire?" J smiled up at her and pulled her down onto his knee, his fingers rested on her inner thigh.

"I trust you, but I want this to be a surprise. When we go to London it will just be the two of us, Sam will stay behind on this occasion."

"But she has to take care of me." China's mock protest brought a smile to his lips and they both chuckled as Sam stalked unnoticed from the room.

"You'd better go and get ready for work," J laughed as he lifted her from his knee, "China…" She turned to look at him. "China, I do love you," he said softly bringing a smile to her face.

"I love you too, Master." In an instant she was kissing him before jogging into the bathroom to change.

J sat at the table, picked up pen and paper and wrote an acceptance to the opening, this would be the first gathering he had attended for six months, his first with China.

SEVENTEEN

Sam placed the boxes on the bed and pulled off the lids, for the last ten days the two subs had talked about little else than the gallery opening. China was both excited and apprehensive about their trip; she wanted everybody to see how well she served J, well aware that she would be watched for the slightest indiscretion.

Now that the day had arrived she felt sick at the merest thought of all those people looking at her, she became sure that she would let J down in every way. The boxes containing her outfit had remained closed and fastened tight since Sam had returned with them, even the young submissive didn't know what was inside. It felt like Christmas, both women eager to see inside. For a few days Sam had sulked when she had found out she would not be going but that had subsided into excitement for China.

As the clock ticked closer and closer to five o'clock it was almost too much to bear; finally J allowed her to get ready and like an excited child China had grabbed the boxes and disappeared into the bedroom.

Rather than fight the tight knot securing the box she simply took the nail scissors and cut it – both China and Sam held their breath as the lids came off. Wrapped in tissue paper each garment was carefully lifted and placed on the bed, almost daring not to be revealed. With shaking hands China slowly peeled back the fine paper to reveal her outfit.

The top was a deep green – she had never seen anything quite like it. By all appearances it should have been a corset, the cups lifted her breasts and held them in soft leather. Fine silver threads had been woven into the ridges and gave it an armoured effect that shimmered in the light when she moved. Above the main section, which gripped and held her breasts and torso, was a fine mesh that at a first glance appeared to be black, but was in fact a slightly darker green that gave the wearer the appearance of wearing a green body stocking under the ornate bodice. She uncovered new stockings and shoes, the heels of which pushed up her calves and gave more shape to her legs. Finally she uncovered a deep green dress that flowed down to her ankles. Slowly she turned over every leaf of paper.

"What are you looking for?" Sam asked, joining in the hunt for something she didn't have a clue was.

"There are no knickers!"

"No, tonight you will not wear any." J's voice cut through the rustling of paper and made both ladies stand bolt upright. "When you prepare her tonight, Sam, I want you to shave her completely. Only her face is to be made up and then I want you to bring her into my study once she is prepared. Understand?"

Sam nodded her head and carefully laid each individual garment on the bed, she packed away the boxes and cleaned up the paper until the room was tidy.

"Go and run the bath, my pet." China instructed. When the girl had left China turned her attention to J, "I will make you proud of me tonight."

He crossed the room and turned her around, snaking his arms around her waist and holding her tightly. His lips kissed her shoulder, "I have always been proud of you, my love. I have been too selfish and kept you locked up here."

China reached up and ran her nails through his hair, turning her head to kiss his lips.

"No, Master. You have not been selfish, you have given me more than I could have dreamed of, a life I needed."

"You are such a pretty butterfly, you deserve to be seen," he replied, his mouth pulled back slightly from hers. She strained upwards to kiss him but he pulled away, "Time for you to go and get ready."

As she left the room he patted her buttocks and watched her leave before opening the wardrobe and retrieving his own outfit.

China looked in the mirror, tears filled her eyes and she fought back the salt water. Sam's preparation of her make-up was perfect and she wondered if the girl had been practicing. Without being told she had bent between her Mistress's legs and carefully painted J's mark upon the silk soft thigh.

"Thank you," China choked, she pulled Sam forward in a warm embrace and cuddled her affectionately, "best go get my clothes."

The younger woman did as she was told, returning with each article in turn. China wanted to steal a look as she dressed but decided against it, she didn't want to spoil the effect and it was only when Sam had placed the last shoe on her foot that she turned to look in the mirror.

"You look so beautiful, Ma'am," Sam told her. Shock stretched across China's face and she wasn't sure if she was looking at her own reflection.

"God… Do you think he will be pleased?" she dared to ask.

"If he isn't then he is already dead, Ma'am."

Slowly China walked through the house and gently knocked on the study door. When she was told to enter she saw J sitting at the computer working. He made her wait for a moment before he looked up. He didn't say a word but she could see from the expression on his face that he was struck by her appearance. He stood and fished a small box from the draw.

"Please turn around and close your eyes," he requested, China did so reluctantly.

She felt his fingers draw around her neck and expected to feel leather against her skin, instead cold metal made her shiver.

"Open your eyes and look in the mirror," he told her. China walked into the bathroom again and Sam's face lit up in a bright smile. Quickly China stepped in front of the mirror and closed her eyes. When she did dare open them a decorative silver chain graced her throat. Its beauty and simplicity was matched only by the splendour of its owner.

She almost ran through the house to J, throwing her arms around his neck and kissing him hungrily. "I love you, Master," she giggled happily, planting kisses around his mouth before pulling away.

"I think we are ready." J pulled on his jacket and led her down to the waiting car. As they climbed in China glanced up at the window and waved slightly to Sam. This was her time and she was going to enjoy every moment of it.

Paul stood and looked out across the garden, his lips gripped his cigar and he held out his arm.

"You must have a million questions for me, let's walk." China stretched her legs before joining him on her feet, she placed her arm through his and they started to roam the gardens. Neither of them spoke, China hoped he would not shatter her thoughts of J.

"Your Master had a gift, although it was a gift that many did not recognise; the ability to train without cruelty, without malice." Paul explained. It was a statement that China knew only too well. She had felt the destructive element of being trained by a malicious and inexperienced Dom and it was not a regime she wished to revisit in a hurry.

"I saw you once, across the room at one of the final parties you both attended. You looked so radiant, so confident by his side, but by then J and I no longer spoke and it would have been awkward so I left before he realised I was there."

China wanted to look at him; she felt the urge to slap him but decided against it. "Who can blame you, so many of his 'friends' abandoned him in the end; the calls, the invites, dwindled until I think he felt he could only rely on myself and Sam."

Paul stopped, he sucked in hard on the cigar and tossed it away, the smoke trickled from his lips and China was sure that his eyes were glazing over.

"You are no more to blame than the others." She gripped his arm tightly to let him know he wasn't alone.

"No, but I was the one person who should have know better. The one person he should have depended upon and instead I was one of the first to walk away." Paul was punishing himself with the startling confession and China was not going to make it easy for him.

"Yes you did, you took the easy option and your friend almost died alone," she stated. Paul let go of her arm and walked towards the lake. He looked long and hard at the water, swans elegantly drifted passed, their beady black eyes peering at him accusingly for a moment before they felt he was beneath them and they sailed away.

"I wonder if he would forgive me if he were here now?" China took his arm again and hugged him.

"He probably wouldn't. Your fault was being human; his fault was being stubborn and totally Dom. If it's any consolation I forgive you." She reached up and gently kissed his cheek before leaving him to stand on the edge alone.

Bright lights blasted the pavement in front of the gallery as they stepped from the car, stragglers waited by the door in the vein hope they would be allowed in.

Occasionally a familiar face would push through the crowd, flash an invite and enter. J sat rigid in his seat, his fingers gripped China's hand tightly. She stared into his pale face, his brown beard had been shaved down to follow the lines of his cheeks and mouth; he reached into his jacket pocket and pulled on a pair of sunglasses, the lens fitted his eye-sockets perfectly and placed a black wall between his eyes and the outside world, allowing him to watch the room without them knowing it.

The door popped open and the organisers looked inside – China wasn't sure which of them they recognised but they were swiftly ushered in without waiting. Inside the room was a cavern, great canvases had been suspended from fragile looking cable, white and blue walls glared out almost blindingly. Amateurish works of art mixed with highly professional pieces, sculptures decorated the floor in a highly disorganised way, "It must have taken them hours to organise." J whispered into China's ear, she tried not to giggle.

Scanning the room she saw Mary – the thunderbolt hit her and in desperation she tried to pull away. J held her tight and pulled her close, drawing her into his body protectively.

"Remember who you are here with, China." His voice was calm and protective but she felt her knees going weak at the thought of the betrayal Mary had levelled against her.

"Can we go?" she heard herself plead but J had already taken her hand and led her towards a corner.

"Who is your Master?" he asked.

"You are, you are my Master." His voice was leading her back to his dominance, China was returning to her personality, burying the timid Gill beyond reach.

J felt the tightness in his chest and gripped the wall, searing pain filled the left hand side of his body and he almost fell, this time it was China's turn to support him.

"Master, you are stronger than this, you rise above them. Now is not the time to fail," she told him and using all her strength guided him down into a chair and fished inside his pocket for his pills. Not wishing her Master to be seen taking them China sipped a glass of wine and palmed the two small pills into her own mouth, she knelt, kissed his hand and then pressed her lips to his, passing the pills into his mouth with a dribble of wine. Surprise hit him and J pulled away and swallowed quickly but as the pain started to ease he smiled at China and stroked her face with the palm of his hand. It was a familiar sign of affection that she had come to love, it made her feel small, protected, and loved.

"J, good to see you again, glad you could come," a hand had been thrust down at the pair and it caught them a little off guard. When China looked up she did so into the round face of an Indian looking gentleman.

"Hello, Gareth. You will excuse me for not standing but I think I am on the verge of a heart attack," J stated. China held her breath and wondered what the man would do. To her relief he roared with laughter.

"Always the kidder. J, good to see you here, almost given you up for dead." The man pulled his hand back placed it into his hip pocket. "To be honest this all looks a little dull and I came to ask if you fancied popping down to my place next weekend. I have a young thing that is running wild and could do with some teaching."

China watched the man's cheeks puff red, his eyes darted left and right in case somebody was listening. "Bring your young lady if you like… Sorry dear, didn't catch your name."

"China, pleased to meet you."

"She is my… she is the person I have waited my whole life for," J cut in, it was the first declaration China had heard him make about her status and it shocked her a little.

"Really, must be something special. You'd better bring her down." Gareth said stepping back slightly so that he could give China the once over, "I'm sure we can keep her amused."

The man shuffled off towards a group of men in the corner who seemed to ignore the art in favour of admiring the waitresses, China watched

Gareth talking to them in hushed tones and then one by one they looked in her direction, China was sure she was being discussed.

"They will come over gradually, in ones and twos and introduce themselves in the hope of meeting you. Like flies round a honey pot they will try to gain your attention and the very first time you leave my side at least one of them will try to take you from me," J explained. China knelt by his side and placed her wrists in the small of her back.

"The runt of the group is a man named Peter Martin; he is a brutal man when alone with a woman. If he is true to form he will wait until you go into the bathroom and therefore out of sight before he strikes up a conversation with you. He will rely on your training to ensure you pay him attention." As J spoke China noted each man's size and build – she singled Martin out almost straight away. His jet black hair had been slicked back and he looked like a 1940's spiv, the suit he wore looked expensive, as did the gold watch on his wrist.

"Don't be fooled by the exterior, he was born with wealth and daddy gives him just enough to stay at arm's length. The suit he wears is off the peg, the watch is fake – as is his tan." China looked back at J and studied his face, he was facing the wrong direction to be able to see the group and yet he described Martin perfectly.

"What do you wish me to do if he does as you have described, Master?" China asked – it was all she could do to drag her eyes away from the group, it aroused her to know the effect she was obviously having on them.

"Mr Martin has a slight problem with premature ejaculation. I want you to take him to one side and see if it's true; simply tell him about your session at Madam Sophia's."

"If it pleases you, Master," China smiled mischievously. "And then what shall I do?"

"You will come back to me and retake your position. Back where you belong."

China crossed the floor and slipped between the guests, she took the long route to make sure that the group of men saw her, in particular Martin with whom she flashed an innocent smile.

She was aware that he watched her enter the narrow corridor and when she emerged from the toilet she was not surprised to see him waiting.

"I understand that you are one of J's girls," he sneered, his thin fingers grasping his tumbler tightly.

"That is correct Sir. Master J has been good enough to train me; I do everything to please him." China informed him, Martin steered her towards a doorway and expertly guided her into it, cutting off any means of escape. Deep inside China wanted to laugh out loud, J had predicted it so perfectly.

"J is looking a little tired, it all seems to be getting a bit much for him. Maybe, if you would like, you might want to come and stay for me. Give him a bit of rest... would you like that?" His eyes shot from her eye-line to her cleavage. If she had been alone she would have felt quite intimidated and would probably rushed away, or poured a drink over him at least. Here she had known what to expect and was sure that her Master was watching over her, looking up she saw she was right. J had positioned himself on the narrow walkway of upper level and could see exactly what was going on.

"Has he trained you well? He hardly seems able these days, poor fellow."

"Yes Sir, although sometimes he sends me to Madam Sophia for more intense training." China lied. Martin was openly leering and she could tell he was only interested in the details.

"The little dress maker?" He was getting uncomfortably close and China could smell his stale breath – she wanted to push past him and go to her Master but she remembered his instructions. Taking a deep breath she leaned forward giving Martin a clear view down her top and got her mouth close to his ear; she blew gently, aware of the effect it was probably having before starting her story. She positioned her leg between his, the flat of her thigh rested against his groin and she could feel her influence on him. Already the bulge in his trousers was semi-hard as she started to relate in fine detail the events of her private encounter at Madam Sophia's shop.

Before long Martin had placed his hands on the wall either side of China's body and was breathing erratically, so much so that China was sure he was the one about to have a heart attack. She decided it was time to finish the game and rubbed his groin with her thigh as she finished off her story.

"I couldn't move at all, they punished me so severely that my poor bottom was numb for days and then they made me crawl to Madam. She was sitting in this big chair, her legs up on the arms and do you know what they made me do?" she asked innocently. Martin gave out a grunt and told he to continue, his fingers openly rubbed his crotch against her, revulsion crept into China's throat.

"They made me lick her sweet lips until she climaxed all over my face. Do you think that was naughty Mr Martin? And Master never punished them, you would have, wouldn't you, Sir?" She hid her disgust behind the most naïve voice she could muster.

Martin grunted and his head came up for a moment before he let out a sigh of pained relief. High above J shook his head and smiled before walking away towards the stairs.

"Oh Sir, you are all damp!" China ran her fingers over the wet patch that had formed through the man's trousers, his face scratched scarlet and he tried desperately to cover it with his jacket.

"Thank you for your kind offer, but it seems you have a little problem of your own to sort out before you can hope to handle a submissive like me."

Ducking under his arms China pecked him on the cheek and hurried off to find J.

She found him just in time to witness the letch making his excuses and leaving. China stared into the darkness of the glasses covering J's eyes.

"Poor Mr Martin, he didn't stay long."

"No, my sweet China. I guess men like him just come and go; in his case very quickly." He took her hand and kissed it softly before whispering, "I am very proud of you, my China."

When he sat China knelt on the floor between his legs, J's hand rested reassuringly on her shoulder, his fingers massaging her smooth skin. China was lost in her own world and didn't notice Mary standing in front of them.

"J, I see you and Gill are together, that's nice." China looked up into her face, she refused to react but waited patiently for her Master to reply.

"China is my submissive, and yes she is very much a part of my life. Are you alone?" J made a show of looking around the room to see if anyone was waiting for her.

"Yes I am quite alone these days." Mary answered, her eyes never leaving China.

"I want to congratulate you on the success of your opening, it seems to be going well." His words seemed lost on her. Without saying a word Mary knelt in front of China, her trembling hand touched the submissive's thigh but China simply turned away.

"I wanted to tell you how sorry I am, I never meant to hurt you. You are my best friend." Mary said slowly, she tried desperately to look China in the eye, "Please, come back to us as Gill, this isn't you. How can you bare to be this way?"

The words dug deep into China's thoughts and she considered her response, finally she stared directly at her former friend.

"You are very wrong; this is exactly the person I was always meant to be. I must thank you for being a catalyst in my transformation, without your betrayal I would never have become China," the words sent tears streaming down Mary's face and she quickly stood and rushed to the toilet. J leaned forward, his mouth stopped a hair's breath from China's ear.

"Now it is time for you to take your revenge, go to her, seduce her, and make her yours." He pulled away and drank heavily from the glass in his hand.

"I don't understand, Master."

"It is very simple, she begged for forgiveness and you refused, now you must release her from torment and that can only happen through penance." His words sounded familiar and China understood what Sam must have gone through.

The bathroom seemed a little oppressive compared to the vast expanse of space in the gallery and China walked along the wall pressing the cubicle doors. Each one was empty until she touched the final door, it refused to budge and she knocked gently.

"I'll be out in a minute." Mary sniffed; the sound of paper being torn from the roll echoed slightly and she knocked again. The latch was pulled back and Mary blinked out at her, but before she could react properly China had pushed her back inside and slipped the bolt into a locked position.

"You want my forgiveness?" she asked sternly, Mary nodded and tried to embrace her. "Then you will have to earn it. On your knees." For a moment Mary looked confused, the cubicle was narrow and cramped but eventually she slipped down onto her knees.

"Good, you must do as you are told – hands behind your back." China instructed and slowly Mary did as she was told. Once she was in the correct position China unbuttoned her blouse and slipped her hand inside her former friend's bra. The older woman couldn't stop herself from moaning softly, she pushed her breasts up to meet China's toying fingers.

"What will you do to earn my forgiveness?" China questioned gripping Mary's dark red hair and snapping her head back.

"Anything… I miss you so much, Gill." The slap that crossed Mary's face bounced around the walls and caused the victim to cry out in pain and shock.

"What is my name?"

"China, your name is China." Mary cried out as China gripped her hair tightly.

"Good, I thought you would be pleased by what I have become," China mocked. "After all you it was you that really introduced me to the scene fully."

"Look at you; you've become a monster – broken by that twisted man," Mary countered. "It was a kick, a thrill to feel his control. You weren't supposed to be brainwashed into staying that way!"

China released her grip, her fingers took the edges of her skirt and gradually the material slipped up her thighs. Like a rabbit caught in the headlights of a speeding car Mary couldn't move, the hard floor dug into her knees but still she couldn't resist watching China reveal herself. As more and more of China's legs were uncovered Mary felt all her willpower slipping away.

"Do you like my shoes?" China asked. Mary could do little but nod in agreement. "I think they are so nice you should kiss them." China lifted her leg and placed it on her victim's chest, her hands gripped either side of the cubicle and she waited expectantly. A little unsure of herself Mary lifted the shoe to her mouth and placed a single kiss on the top. She didn't move away, instead she remained motionless as China inched the hem of her dress further and further up to reveal her bare thigh and exposed cunt.

"You like that, don't you?" Once again Mary nodded at the question. Her body felt numb and weak, her vocal cords seemed to have dried up to the point where she could no longer talk. "You want me!"

It was a statement of fact. Suddenly China knew how her Master had been able to tell so much about people, instinct. The woman before her was reacting in subtle ways, ways that gave her away to the trained eye and was maybe not even aware she was doing. China was still sure that J was highly empathic but he also knew people, he had studied them.

"You may kiss my thigh." This time Mary shook her head at the instruction, hesitating she pulled back.

"No, I'm not like that." She moaned, her eyes kept darting up to China's before moving her gaze back between her legs, it settled on the perfect impression of J's mark.

"Kiss Master J's mark, show your respect," cautiously the kneeling victim bent forward to kiss the ink, when she was close China reached out and held the woman's head before she had the opportunity to slip away as she gingerly kissed the soft flesh containing the mark – China noted the kiss lingered more than it could have, the reciprocator moved and Mary found herself tantalisingly close to China's wet lips.

"If you want my forgiveness then you will please me," China stated, she gripped Mary's head and refused to let her go until she got what she wanted; a smile stretched across her lips as a soft mouth touched her sensitive skin followed by a nervously probing tongue.

As Mary knelt she was flooded with emotions, she was confused because although she felt sick and repulsed by what she was doing she couldn't stop, she looked up at China and searched the dominate woman's face for a sign that she was to stop, but China's eyes were closed and her free hand was stroking the top of her breast through the fine mesh of her top; her breath seemed heavy and occasionally she sighed out loud when Mary guessed she had touched the right spot. Her knees were sore and her back was in agony and when she paused for a second China pulled away. "Very nice, but maybe I should show you how it's done... Stand up and get up on the toilet, sit on the cistern," China instructed, slowly Mary did as she was told.

"What did I do wrong?" Mary questioned.

"You licked me in the same way most men do, rough and unthinking," came the reply, Mary blushed. It was true, her only experience of oral sex had come from a man and she had no other experience to learn from, she remembered how it had been a shambling precursor to sex that had left her frustrated and bored.

Perched on the toilet she felt exposed, she bit her lips and closed her eyes to the scene that was unfolding before her; Mary started to feel hot flushes spark and spread across her body.

China kissed the woman's leg and ran her hands up and under her dress, her nails raked Mary's thighs, digging in just enough to make her friend react. Once her hands reached the tops of Mary's thighs China started to kiss, planting tiny, innocent kisses along the wake of her nails. Mary placed her head against the water pipe coming down from the roof and gave herself completely over to the strange sensations her body was enjoying, already her nipples had hardened but now they ached to be touched and she unbuttoned her bra with trembling fingers. When she proceeded to touch her full breasts China reached up and slapped her hands away.

"You will wait for me to allow you to touch yourself, do you understand?" Mary complained with her eyes and nodded slightly, China returned to where she had left off.

When she reached the top of Mary's thigh China used the tip of her tongue, it stroked and caressed, explored the crease between thigh and crotch, forcing Mary to pull back even more until she sat bolt upright and was unable to move. She wore a thong and China smiled mischievously, her tongue licked its way across the smooth material and she felt the folds of Mary's sex, the hot lips gave themselves away and when she found the centre China pushed with the flat of her tongue. The movement was explosive and sent Mary into shock; quickly China narrowed her tongue and pressed where she guessed she would find the clit. When she did Mary stopped breathing and China pulled away slightly. "Breathe," she whispered, the smile reappeared as her partner started to breathe slowly and deeply.

"Please, Gill. Don't stop," she hissed, but at the sound of her former name China did stop and she pulled away. Confused Mary sank down and gripped her shoulders.

"Please, don't stop. What did I do wrong? Tell me," she implored, "tell me what I did wrong so I don't do it again."

"My name is China; do not insult me by using my former name. It is a symbol of what I was, not what I am," China spat. She wanted to turn away, to go back to J and ask him to take her home where she was safe from her past, but instead she took a harder edge.

"Turn around and put your hands either side of the pipe. Spread your legs as far as they will go," China ordered. Willingly Mary did as she was instructed. Because of the cistern she was bent forward pushing her buttocks out and China guided her down until she was almost at a forty-five degree angle. Effortlessly she peeled back Mary's dress and revealed her buttocks, China teased her by running her long fingers up the back of Mary's thigh before guiding them between her legs and pressing hard against the material covering her cunt for a second.

SMACK, the impact of her hand against Mary's buttocks was instant and unexpected, it sent China's victim crying out in pain and shock. The white of her cheeks had already started to redden as China struck again, this time Mary remained quiet. Four blows later and China felt her own hand starting to numb from the punishment she had exacted, she ran her other hand over the red blotches of her handiwork and enjoyed the heat being given off. She slipped down onto the closed lid of the toilet and buried her head between Mary's legs from behind, as she started to gently lick her way along the thongs path she felt Mary pushing back onto her tongue. The heat that met China's tongue equalled that of Mary's bruised cheeks. China reached up and wrapped the elastic waistband of the thong around her fingers and pulled it up sharply for a second before sliding it down as far as she could. When China was stopped from going further by the wearers spread legs, Mary reached down and in a grunt of frustration ripped them off. The lifeless remnants fell in tatters down her legs and stopped at her shoes; China grinned inside and leaned forward. Her fingers gripped Mary's thighs tightly and she returned to pushing with her tongue, she followed the line between anus and vagina with the very tip of her tongue before flattening it again and pressing Mary's labia, massaging it from behind.

"Jesus Christ," came the reaction – pleased at the success of her aims China continued, relentlessly working deep inside Mary's sex before pulling out and continuing the massage of her outer lips.

Suddenly Mary started to buck, she pressed hard against the wall and pushed her body back onto China's mouth, she cried out in pleasure as her orgasm hit, the rolling pleasure that caught her off guard weakened her arms and legs, she buckled and gripped the pipe for support as China curled her tongue and allowed the sweet juice to roll into her mouth where she held it. The force of the climax caused Mary to sob; her head remained buried in her forearms as she tried to control her body. China stood and pulled back on her friends hair until her wet cheeks showed, she leaned forward and kissed the woman's trembling lips, forcing the nectar into her mouth. Mary swallowed hard as China pulled away, she kissed her index finger and placed it onto Mary's swollen lips, "Now you are forgiven. Goodbye."

Before China left the toilet she smoothed down her outfit and re-applied her make-up in the mirror. In the cubicle she could hear the Mary's gentle sobbing; she smiled to herself and made her way back to J without a second thought.

"You look like the cat that got the cream." J stated as she knelt back between his legs.

"I did, Master, I am."

EIGHTEEN

China sat on the edge of the bed and slowly packed her case; she had removed her party outfit and wrapped it back in tissue paper. She gathered the few possessions she had brought with her and put them away – the only thing she kept out were her travelling clothes and the collar J had given her. Just sitting there she hoped to hear J's voice; as her fingers unbuckled the catch to the collar she wanted desperately to hear his disapproval, nothing was forthcoming and when she had completed the task she slipped it into the side pocket of her case.

"I wonder if you really were proud of me?" she said aloud. The top of the case closed and she dressed quickly. Outside the sound of the dinner party seemed to get louder and for a moment and she froze, listening before pulling on her clothes. As she eased on her new stockings there was a faint tapping on her door, with her heart in her mouth China opened it a little; the master of the house's submissive stood with her hands behind her back, head bowed, waiting.

"I missed you, I wondered where you were."

China pulled her inside the room quickly, checked the corridor and then locked the door. "I'm leaving, do you understand?" she explained, the girl nodded and flopped down on the bed.

"Can I ask you a question, China?" she asked quietly, her fingers played with her nails nervously.

"Of course."

"Have you ever been in love with anyone apart from your Master?" It seemed an odd question to ask but China answered.

"I have loved many times, but never as intensely or as fully as with my Master. Why do you ask?" She ran her fingers through the girl's hair to comfort her.

"I think I am falling in love with you."

The words came out of the blue and China paused for a moment; she sat down on the bed next to the girl and took her hands in hers.

"Love comes in many forms, your see me as a strong woman, a dominant maybe, but I am not for you. You will learn that, as your training progresses, you will come into contact with many men and women just like me…"

"I already have, but you have touched me in a way none of the others have." the girl cut in. "They seem to treat this as a game, but this is who I am, what I am."

China laughed out loud, they were words she had used to justify her way of life in the past and now this slip of a girl had done exactly the same. China pulled her close and kissed her affectionately, "I will be around, you will see me from time to time and I will check on your progress." She stood and took the handle of her case and pulled it upright.

"When will I see you again?" the novice asked. She joined China in standing and took the case. "Promise me we will see each other again."

"I promise, I just can't say when." China opened the door and led the way down towards the front door, when she opened it she saw Paul leaning against his car.

"Thought you might need a lift home," he said pulling the boot open and easing China's case inside; he ran his fingers down her face in a way that haunted her from the past.

"Why are you doing this – because I won't be your sub?" China asked directly.

"I know, but it seems we have a lot to talk about. I missed out on the last part of my best friend's life whereas you were with him. I'd like you to share those memories with me." China looked into his eyes for a catch.

"I wonder if you're a psychiatrist?" she said out loud.

"Actually I lecture in psychology." His answer made China laugh out loud, it was the first time she had done so since J's death.

Paul started the car and slipped it into gear, they pulled away and in the rear view mirror China watched the little novice disappear into the night.

The trip home was filled with a warm silence, China rested her head in her Master's lap, her hands gripped his leg – if she had been a cat she was sure she would have been purring in her contentment. Gently J stroked her hair as she lay across him, outside people staggered through the streets and he enjoyed watching them, lost in their own worlds. Occasionally they would pass couples laughing, arguing, talking and he would wonder what scenario was being played out in their vanilla world.

"Master, may I ask a question?" China said as she rolled onto her back to look up at him, J ran his finger across her forehead.

"Anything."

"How long have you known that you were a Dom?" her question was filled with wonder, she felt the need to learn more about the man sharing the rest of his life with her.

"All my life, sweet China; but I started to explore at seventeen and I made my mistakes, some good, some bad." There was a mixture of joy and pain on J's face.

"You need to see the doctor on Monday, Master." China was concerned, the pain he had felt during the evening was more intense than she had ever seen him endure and although it could have been the stress of the opening it might have been a precursor of something bigger.

The remainder of the journey was silent. At home China shared her experience with a wide eyed Sam, the younger woman eager to know everything that had occurred. Finally China paused; she looked down at her drink and sought an answer as to whether or not to tell Sam about J's attack, she eventually came to a decision.

"Sam, you know the Master is very ill?" She watched Sam's face carefully.

"Yes. You told me to keep an eye on him and to make sure he eats and rests, takes his medication when he has to. I promise I have been doing all that."

"Well," the words stuck in China's throat a little, "tonight he had some kind of seizure, it only lasted a few minutes but I was very worried."

"I promise he has been eating, and when I take him the pills I wait whilst he takes them, honest." Sam's voice was full of concern not only for the health of their Master but also that China might have felt she had failed in her duty.

"I think this is deeper than everyday things, I get the impression that he will be leaving us soon. Damn it why won't he fight harder?" China slammed her glass down on the table and sent Sam reeling backwards in fright, tears of frustration welled in her eyes. "Why won't he fight?"

"I am fighting, I told you I would." the words made China spin around and she faced the door.

"Then fight harder, this isn't fair. We haven't spent enough time together and you are going to leave us alone. We, I need, you." Defiantly she faced him.

"But some things are inevitable; we cannot stop this as much as we cannot stop the grains of time."

"Don't you dare get so fucking Zen on me now, I am serious. There has to be something they can do," she sobbed. J held out his hand and she ran to him, his big arms wrapped her tight, her chest buried in his. Tears soaked into his robe and he did his best to comfort her. Gently he kissed the top of her head and kept her safe.

"You know we have explored every option, now it's just a matter of time," her sobbing grew more intense and he simply held her until she became limp in his arms.

He half carried, half guided her into the bedroom and undressed her. Sam watched and carefully arranged China's clothes on the chair as J handed them to her. China's fingers gripped the pillows and she dug her face into the covers like a child afraid of the dark.

She felt J climb into the bed beside her, his hand snaked across her hips and he pulled close. As he kissed her shoulder China rolled over, her breasts pressed against him, hungrily she kissed his mouth and ran her fingers down his back. When J responded China rolled him onto his back and kissed his chest, her teeth grazed his nipples and he arched his back, willing her on.

Digging her nails into the hairs on his chest China closed her lips around his nipple and suckled, her teeth pulled at the pink flesh. J pulled at her hair as pleasure raged through his body, he wanted to feel her, to become one with her but this was out of his control and he tried to pull away. China refused and fought back, her long fingers slipped under the covers and gripped his cock, it was already hardening and she could feel the veins throbbing against her hand. Gently she slipped across, her legs straddled him and her fingers started to work their way up and down his hard cock.

J moaned out loud and placed his hands on the headboard, he lifted her from the bed using the power of his legs and the only way China could stay on was to dig her nails hard into his chest. She slipped down, her legs gripped his calf muscles and she rubbed her breasts against his cock. "Do you want me, Master?" She kissed his stomach as she asked her question, his cock seemed to get harder and he rubbed back and forth gently.

"I want you more than anything in my life," J moaned. China smiled and moved further down resting her lips against the tip of his cock for a moment and gently sucked. The softness of her lips and the gentle way she flicked her tongue over the surface made J grip the bed and push up towards her.

Just when China was sure that her Master was getting used to the treatment he was receiving she ran her tongue down the underside of his cock until she found his balls. J relaxed and enjoyed the adrenaline pumping through his veins, the mischievous glint appeared in China's and she took one of his balls between her lips; slowly she started to hum. China's face lit up when she saw the effect that her actions had on J, his hands shot down to the sheets and he gripped them firmly.

"God you're good," J hissed fighting the urge to climax and shook the fog from his mind. He reach down and pulled gently at her arm – almost unwilling to let go of her prize China stayed where she was for the moment until using both hands J eased her up the bed. She lay on his chest looking into his eyes for a while; she traced the outline of his beard and teased his mouth with her nail. She loved the shape of his nose, it seemed to be chiselled into his features. Finally China forced herself to kneel up, her hand reached back and slowly played with his cock to keep it hard; she leaned forward slightly, her breasts hanging down close to his mouth and as J started to suck from them hungrily she eased his throbbing length inside her aching cunt. Savouring every inch China moved back slowly until he was fully inside her, he felt the heat of her muscles rippling against him and leaned back a fraction to push a little bit further inside; his balls now rubbed her lips sending spasms of pleasure through her body.

"I wish I had met you ten years ago," she groaned as rhythmically J started to make love to her. It was not as frantic as her previous encounters with opposite sex – J seemed to measure each of his actions to completely satisfy his partner. As she watched him her head lolled to one side, his hands cupped her breasts and his thumbs started to torment her nipples with small, tight circles around her areola. Where once he would concentrate on one at a time he now was in a position to manipulate both and it only served to make China wetter.

For what appeared to be hours they moved and twisted, changed position and played, Master and sub changed dominant role so many times neither seemed to have an advantage. As daylight started to break J slipped his hand down her spine, China lay flat on his chest, her breasts seemed to have glued to his, sweat coated them both and as her sex started to spasm he eased his finger between her cheeks. As it pressed her anus China collapsed under the force of the orgasm that filled her and seconds later J's cock erupted deep inside her. China's legs gripped his, it felt so good that she didn't want the experience to end, she rocked back and forth pressing his balls as if to milk as much from him as possible.

They became one being, bodies entwined in a tangle of pleasure and desire, they breathed together and neither wanted to move in case the spell was broken. When Sam finally came in to wake China for work she found them both asleep, China still draped across her Master's chest.

"Tell me about your tattoos," Paul asked as he drove, one hand resting on the wheel the other on open window.

"I wanted to show Master how much he meant to me, how much he owned me."

"Yes, but when did you decide?" he pushed. They entered village after village, passing through quickly before China could note their names. She eased back into the seat and thought for a moment, closing her eyes in recollection.

The doctor walked into the kitchen and asked Sam to leave. China nodded and waited for the young sub to exit.

"I take it that it isn't good news, Doctor." He placed his bag on the table and took out a bottle of pills.

"I can't give you a time period, by all rights he should be dead by now but those will help with the pain. I doubt he will take them but you never know."

China escorted him out and went to find Sam, she was helping J to sit up in bed. He crossed his legs and although the pain was unbearable China could see he was starting to try and meditate – without saying a word she motioned for Sam to leave the room and eagerly the younger woman did as she was instructed. Once out of earshot China pulled Sam close and whispered into her ear.

"I am going to see Madam Sophia, if Master asks where I am you will tell him I have gone to the chemist for the doctor, understand?" Sam nodded and peeked around the door.

"I don't think he will be asking questions too soon but what do I do if he wants to get up?"

China kissed her cheek, "Keep him in bed, he needs the rest now."

The drive into town was short, traffic seemed to have disappeared. China was able to park in front of Sophia's door and she knocked lightly. When one of the girls came to the door China pushed it open far enough for the girl to see she was alone. Inside Beatrice knelt in front of one of Sophia's clients, as soon as she recognised China she smiled.

"I must see Madam urgently," the expression on China's face was stern and Beatrice sent the other girl off to find their Mistress.

"What is wrong China?" Beatrice asked. China looked at the woman standing in the centre of the room and shook her head, Beatrice nodded and remained silent until Sophia pulled back the curtains and stepped into the light.

"May I speak to you in private, Madam?" China requested, the girls looked for instruction from their Mistress and she nodded.

"Come into the back, we can take a drink and you can tell me why you are here without an appointment, or your Master."

She led the way back into the recesses of the shop – away from the main façade it seemed very ordinary. Peeling wallpaper lined the corridor and Sophia seemed to be genuinely embarrassed by it.

"Forgive the décor, we have not had a chance to convert the rest of the building yet," she explained, opening a side door to a grand office that rivalled Master J's.

"I came because I do not know who else to ask," China started; she felt uncomfortable asking another Domme for help. "I wish to carry my Master's mark permanently and you are his dress maker, and confidant."

Blushing Sophia poured them both a drink and handed China a glass, she thought for moment. "When do you wish for this to happen?"

"As soon as possible, you know my Master is gravely ill and I wish to do it tonight, if it is possible."

Sophia thought for a moment, her fingers drummed on her glass and she tapped it against her lips.

"Very well, the man who painted your Master will be with you at eight o'clock sharp. Give him this." Sophia reached into desk draw and pulled out a template. She turned it over in her hands before passing it to China. "Your Master is very special to me, I hope you understand how much you mean to him. My door is always open."

The words seemed so final and China wondered if Madam knew more than she did; China tucked the template into her jacket and thanked the Domme before stealing away before Beatrice could corner her and ask awkward questions.

At eight o'clock China opened the door to find the tattooist waiting, he appeared to have shaved and looked less scruffy. China placed her finger to her lips and he nodded; they walked through the house in total silence until they reached the playroom. Slipping inside China locked the door and finally felt able to speak, "thank you for coming at such a short notice."

"I am glad to get the call, I don't know what your Master did but since I did his job I have been inundated with requests. It was like a seal of approval, the least I can do is come when he asks for me," the man stated, he looked around the room expecting to see J.

"Madam Sophia did not tell you why you are here?"

The man looked a little perplexed, "I didn't think it was for my conversation skills, why don't you explain it to me?"

China walked to the table and picked up the template that Sophia had given her, she ran her fingers over the gothic text before handing it over.

"I want you to mark me with that design," she said, the man rolled the plate over in the palm of his hand.

"Sure, I can do that. Where? Arm? Thigh? Shoulder?"

China bent over the frame J had been fastened onto and placed her hand on her cheeks, "both cheeks."

"Both cheeks? At the same time?" he questioned, China nodded and bent a little further forward.

"Now."

The man started to prepare, choosing the same ink that had been used on J's design. Experimentally he ran his hand over China's smooth cheeks and placed the template in the small of her back.

"You do realise that you ain't going to be able to sit down for a couple of days," he stated as the tip of the needle gun touched her skin.

"Carry on, please," China breathed; the needle pricked her skin and injected the ink, she gripped the metal tightly and gritty her teeth as he went about his work.

Sam cleaned and tended to the scabs surrounding China's tattoo, the man had been right it had been almost unbearable to sit for the last two days but it was worth it. She was aware that Sam openly stared at the markings. "When will you show Master?" she asked when she found her voice;, China thought for a second.

"Tonight, at dinner with the doctor. I shall serve," China smiled, she longed to see J's face when he saw them, she had become very proud of her new decorations since they had been done and now she desperately wanted to show them off.

During the dinner preparations she was careful not to give the game away which was very difficult as J would prowl around the house so quietly that sometimes they forgot he was in. As the time came for the guests to arrive China was able to escape to the bathroom to get ready, leaving Sam to finish off the dinner and greet the guests.

It was largely an informal affair – the kitchen had been set aside and the table cleaned and set for five. The doctor and his wife, their sub, China and J were the only people eating. As they sat around the table China entered and apologised for her delay, she had on a skirt and knew that it would upset J, she shooed Sam from the kitchen subtly and set about serving the diners.

As she passed the top of the table J caught her leg and held her still, "you are wearing a skirt, you know better than that."

Blushing, she turned around and fumbled with the catch at the top, "I have something to show you, Sir. I wanted it to be a surprise." The skirt fell from her waist and on full display the tattoos looked bright and new; applause broke out from the doctor and his wife, their sub bit her lip and her eyes widened in admiration.

148

J sat for a moment and then excused himself – worried that she had angered him China followed him out of the kitchen and into his study.

"Master I am so sorry if I displeased you." She didn't really know what to say. Her hands automatically went to the small of her back, her legs were already open. Suddenly she was filled with the dread that he may release her from his control again.

"China… Sweet China, it is a bit of a shock that is all." When he faced her China could see that tears of pride in his eyes.

"Master, just as you carry my name I wished the world to know who owns me. I don't care who else carries your mark, I wanted you to see that I am willing to be yours totally." She wrapped her arms around him and held him tight.

"I know, and I am very proud and grateful for the sentiment but you will have a long life after I am gone and these marks will not help you find a new Master."

"Then I will do without," China countered. J suddenly fell to the floor and he lay in a heap clutching his chest. In blind panic China ran through the house to the kitchen, dragging the doctor back with her.

"I told you to rest," the doctor said as he helped J to his feet and then supported him back to the bedroom. "Are you going to take these pills?" Through his agony J agreed and swallowed as the pills were literally poured down his throat. His eyes closed almost instantly and the women undressed him and put him to bed.

The doctor watched them work for a moment before taking China to one side, "he should be ok in a couple of days providing he stays in bed. My suggestion is you go to work and give him some peace, Sam can look after him whilst you are out and she can always call me if necessary."

China nodded and bid them all goodnight, waiting until they had gone before she started clearing up; every now and then she would check on her sleeping Master.

NINETEEN

Paul pulled up outside the flat and turned off the engine. He gave it the once over before deciding he liked the look of the place.

"And that was it?"

China fished into her case for the keys to the flat; she ignored the question for as long as possible.

"Did he suffer at the end?" Paul pushed; he needed closure on the matter. "Yes he suffered a great deal, that final day it grew too much for him I think. But then I also think he put it off longer than any of us would."

China stepped from the car and unlocked the door to the flat, she didn't ask Paul in and she was sure he didn't expect to be. As the door closed she leaned back against it and let out a sigh of relief, she was home and it felt good. She closed her eyes and remembered the last day they had been here together.

China unlocked the door and walked into the flat, from the kitchen she could hear the faint sounds of sobbing and followed them.

Sam sat on the chair, her short hair looked unkempt and the make-up had started to run down her cheeks, smudging around her eyes.

"I'm so sorry." She burst out and China placed her hand on the young woman's shoulder.

"Where is he?" she asked, Sam looked up and pointed towards the bedroom.

"Wait here until I come back, did you call the doctor?" Sam shook her head and tried to wipe the salt water from her eyes. "Go and get cleaned up, I will be with Master when you are finished. Bring me some water, a towel and his vodka from the freezer."

Control returned to the house and Sam fell into line – she scuttled off to the bathroom as China unbuttoned her coat and entered the bedroom. At the foot of the bed lay the mattress and covers that made up Sam's bed, China pushed passed them and knelt next to her Master. She ran her fingers across J's forehead and kissed it gently so not to leave a lipstick mark.

His breathing was shallow and he did not open his eyes, sweat ran down his proud face and fell onto the pillow, China used her handkerchief to dry him slightly as she waited for Sam to return – two empty packets of pills lay on the bedside table.

"Don't leave me, Master." She was aware that tears had started to roll down her cheeks even as she fought to hold them back, "I don't want to be alone."

Sam inched into the room and stood with her back against the wall, in her hands she held the water and the vodka, over her thin arm she had draped a towel.

"They are no good over there, bring them here girl." Sam jumped at the command, it was the first time that China had been so harsh and the younger woman found herself shaking as she did as she was told.

"Is he dying?"

"Yes." It was a simple statement that shook Sam to the core and she stood rigid as she looked down at the pale figure on the bed.

"What is he dying of?" The horror on her face said it all and China snatched the towel in disgust.

"Nothing you will catch; now put down those things and get out." Sam did as she was told, relieved to be out in the cool of the corridor.

Gently China lifted J and poured him a glass of vodka As she placed it to his lips and dribbled a little into his mouth he choked for a second before opening his eyes.

"Sweet China." His shaking hand touched her cheek, the end of his nail following the line of tears, "is this for me?"

China nodded; she was scared that if she spoke the words would be lost in a wail of tears.

"You don't have to cry for me…" His breathing was becoming shallower, his eyes rolled as he tried to concentrate, pain stabbed at his face, arms and chest. His legs didn't move and China guessed he was starting to go numb.

"Master please don't leave me, fight for me." She begged; deep inside rage was building up. How dare he leave her now, "Master I love you, what will I do?"

J focused on her pale face, a smile forced its way onto his lips and for a second she thought she saw a trace of the man she loved and respected, "I have nothing left to teach you, my sweet Chin…"

J's eyes flickered for a second, the last few moments of life exhaled and he lay still. For what seemed to be an eternity China sat with his head in her lap, her fingers stroked his hair and beard.

Then, with little ceremony, she bent and kissed his forehead one last time before placing him flat on the bed and tucking the sheet up around him As she stood to leave China picked up the empty packets of pills and slipped them into bottom draw.

"Sam, call the doctor and inform him that the Master appears to have passed away."

China sat in the window of the flat and watched the life on the streets; it all seemed so beneath her now. She was once one of them, she was found, like Sam, and given a second chance at her life. J had taught her everything she needed and yet he had not taught her what came next, what was to become of her.

A gentle cough made her turn to face the door, the doctor waited patiently for her to wake from her thoughts. He had been to the house on many occasions both professionally and as a guest and in his hand he held a small brown envelope.

"Master J left this in my care for when the time came, it is your final set of instructions."

China waved her hand at the table, "Just put them there, I will tend to them later."

"There is one final matter," China looked at him hard. "The empty pill packets, you did dispose of them before the paramedics arrived?"

China nodded; her entire body felt as though it belonged to somebody else, it was cold and numb yet it did not bother her, "you knew he planned to take them all."

"We discussed it but I could never suggest it." He slipped on his coat and took his bag from Sam as she hovered behind him. "Would you like to stay with me, or can I take Sam for a few days?"

"Oh no, please there is so much to do I cannot leave China alone through this," Sam protested.

"Why not, I am going to be alone for a long time to come." China thought simply thanking the doctor and telling him they would be in touch.

As the door closed China realised that another chapter of her life had ended, the future seemed uncertain but then she had often felt that way about the present.

Lightning Source UK Ltd.
Milton Keynes UK
UKOW02f0027130615

253443UK00005B/62/P